ALL THE KING'S MEN

THE BEGINNING

All the King's Men - The Beginning

Published by Phoenix Press

ISBN: 978-1-938991-26-4

Cover art by Reese Dante.

ACKNOWLEDGEMENTS

The more I work with my team of beta readers, the more I realize how incredibly special they are to me and my stories. Without them, the world of AKM would not be what it is today, and it would not be branching into so many wonderful directions. I opened an honest line of communication with them, and every time I send them a draft to critique, I tell them to, "Destroy it, pick it apart." And they do, for which I am eternally grateful, because it allows me to find the magic inside the words I've written, pull it out, and glorify it. So, thank you Elizabeth, Leann, Elvina, Alana, Debra, Kathy, Amanda, Brandy, Gianna, Martha, Ashley, Toni, Sandy, Adriana, Tami, Dawn, and Samantha. You all rock!

BOOKS BY DONYA LYNNE

All the King's Men Series

Rise of the Fallen
Heart of the Warrior
Micah's Calling
Rebel Obsession
Return of the Assassin
All the King's Men - The Beginning

Strong Karma Trilogy

Good Karma
Coming Back to You
Full Circle

Hope Falls Series

Finding Lacey Moon

Stand-Alone M/M Titles

Winter's Fire

Collections and Anthologies

All the King's Men Vol. 1 (books 1-3)
All the King's Men Vol. 2 (books 4-6)
Strong Karma Trilogy Boxed Set
Whispered Beginnings - A Romance Sampler

ALL THE KING'S MEN

THE BEGINNING

DONYA LYNNE

DEDICATION

To you, because I love your story and it deserves
to be told in its entirety.

PREFACE

On March 23, 2012, I published Rise of the Fallen, book one of the All the King's Men Series. At the time, I was a "newbie." I had recently left the realm of online role playing, where my character, Micah, had built up a dedicated following, and wanted to focus my creative energy on turning Micah's online antics and story into a published book. Rise of the Fallen was that story, transcended from the role play medium into published fiction, and it turned out better than I thought it would.

As I made the transition from role play to fiction and dove deeper into Micah's world, an interesting thing occurred. A host of other characters suddenly appeared, all with a story to tell. Those early days of writing Rise came with a slew of split personalities living inside my brain, and some days I couldn't keep up with all of them. Tristan, Arion, Io, Severin, Trace, and Malek were born. Many more have joined the cast since, and still more knock on the door requesting to join on a regular basis, but those were my originals.

After Rise came out and met with overall enthusiastic critical acclaim, I noticed one bit of criticism that came up from time to time in reviews and reader feedback. It seemed that some readers felt they had "missed something." Some even searched book sites to ensure they hadn't missed a book that came out before Rise.

I will admit that, at the time, I still had a lot to learn about writing and story craft. I still do, but now, if I could go back and get a do-over, I would do a better job filling in the gaps of what came before the beginning of Rise of the Fallen.

Then again, I take my cues from my characters, and, at the time, they weren't giving me much about what *did* happen before. For example, Tristan and Josie rarely spoke to me at all about their past, so I had little to say about them. It wasn't until recently (and here it is two years later) that Tristan and Josie finally began talking to me in earnest. And, at the time I wrote Rise, King Bain had not shown himself to me, so I couldn't write about him, either. So, perhaps the series was *supposed* to unfold this way, as ramshackle as that may seem.

Which brings us to the prequel. As I began work on Bound Guardian Angel, which is Trace's story, an explosion of new information about the past engulfed me. I can remember the moment it happened. I felt like a computer downloading an entire databank of material, and when the bulk of it had infiltrated my brain, I actually rocked back in my chair as if I had been shoved and said, "Oh my God! Wow! So, *that's* what happened!" Questions that had sat unanswered in my mind since Rise was published suddenly had answers. And then my friend Jowanna suggested that I write a prequel, and her idea fused with all my new data, and I knew I had to write All the King's Men - The Beginning.

The prequel comes at a perfect time, because the world of AKM is about to shoot in different directions with two sister series in development, as well as a future series called Progeny. Long-held secrets will come to light and we'll see shifting alliances, as well as the emergence of two new paranormal landscapes. But it all begins with the prequel. What you learn here is key to understanding what is yet to come. I hope you enjoy the book.

Thank you,
Donya

THE WAR

2647 BC

Rysk launched himself against the bolted door of his shadow-darkened chamber. The only light came from a single brazier in the far corner. Rysk ached. He ached so deeply…like a sickened human struck by fever and chills, only worse. Much worse. With bruised fists, Rysk beat against the solid wood of the door holding him prisoner. His skin split, but the door held strong, and he shrieked for his mate.

"ABRIAL!" The muscles and tendons in his neck corded as he threw back his head and roared her name.

He had to find a way to escape. To get to her. His *calling* was shredding his sanity, decimating his body, sending him into painful spasms. How could Father lock him away like this, when he knew Rysk's *calling* rent him from the inside out? When the only thing that mattered for him was to return to his mate and sow his seed within her womb. How could his father isolate him and prevent him from being with his beloved Abrial? Where was she now? Was she suffering as much as he was?

"Release me!" Rysk pounded his bloody fists against the thick, oak door, which was bolted from the outside. His throat was raw from shouting, from screeching Abrial's name, and from crying out as pain sliced down his spine and through his limbs. As before, no one answered his cries for help. No one came to free him. The door remained locked.

The room held no windows, as was customary for the daytime chambers of the royal palace. Sunlight was to be avoided at all costs for those like Rysk and his family. Humans had a name for them. *Upir.* Those who avoided the sun, drank blood, and moved like wind.

The *upir* appeared human but weren't. With greater strength and the ability to manipulate human minds, the *upir* were almost godlike to their human counterparts, a race sent to Earth from the stars, to explore and inhabit, according to the ancients who guarded the scrolls in the mountains of faraway lands.

Sunlight scorched *upir* skin. Even the barest exposure caused extreme pain and blistering...even death. Most *upir* were so fearful of the sun that they lived in underground caverns or carved-out caves, but as the son of the race's most affluent family, descended from the first who arrived here long ago, Rysk lived above ground with his parents, older brother, and younger sister.

In his tormented state, Rysk would brave even the sun's light to escape and be with his beloved. He wouldn't get far, but death would be worth the risk if it meant an end to the agony he experienced by being sequestered away from Abrial's touch.

Even now, the brutal, violent spasms were beginning again. Rysk fell to his knees, his body hard, his male flesh throbbing for release within the depths of Abrial's supple warmth, as was his mated right. Why was he being withheld from her? What evil worked against him to keep him from claiming Abrial as his? And she *was* his. She belonged to him. A mated *upir's* rights on such matters were strictly enforced. Then again, no *upir* had ever mated a dreck before. Was that the problem? Was that why he wasn't allowed to see her? Surely, even the drecks—the *upir's* allies, their friends, the ones who helped the *upir* defeat the cruel Dacians—would acknowledge Rysk's right to claim Abrial. They wouldn't deny him, would they? Despite the interracial bond, Premier Argon must have acknowledged the importance of not interfering with his mated rights.

Grimacing through the wracking pain, Rysk's breath came in bursts as every muscle drew tight, pulled taut as if an outside force wished to torture him. His *calling* beseeched him to answer yet again. He looked down at his tunic, which jutted out where his male flesh lifted the fabric away from his body. Just the simple brush of material was enough to bring tears to his eyes as he lifted his tunic away. His member was fully engorged, so red it was almost purple. He knew what he needed to sate this demon, but Abrial wasn't there.

Cringing, he panted as sweat trickled down his face and neck, and he slowly lifted his hand. He ached, but it was such a pleasurable ache. Both arousing and painful.

As soon as his fingers curled around his shaft, both the pleasure and pain ignited, just as he knew it would. His *calling* had already forced itself upon him repeatedly. These episodes had gone on for half a day, and his intermittent deposits dotted the stone floor in dried, clear patches around the room. He hissed, threw his head back, and cried out as yet another powerful release shot out like a mixture of fire and ice to splatter the floor in front of him. He burned for his mate. He needed his Abrial. Now. Before the agony killed him.

KING CATO'S GAZE DARTED TO THE ARCHED DOORWAY of the Great Hall as another cry came from his son's solar chamber. Cato was running out of time. If he couldn't convince Premier Argon—his dreck equivalent and Abrial's father—that Rysk must be allowed to mate Abrial, he would lose Rysk to mated *suffering*, an insanity that would eventually kill Rysk.

Braziers lit throughout the room cast the only light.

"I'm sorry, old friend," Argon said. "But *upir* laws don't apply to us, and Abrial has already been promised to Teo." He held his hands out, palms up, as if there was nothing else he could do.

Cato had to try. Had to *continue* trying. For the sake of his son, he couldn't give up. "Argon, please. My son is dying. If he is not allowed to mate Abrial, I will lose him. Talk to Teo again. I beg you."

A pained, conflicted expression fell over Argon's face as he slumped in the chair across from Cato. "My friend, I've tried. I have spoken to Teo. Several times in fact. He is adamant. His heart is set on having my daughter against any protest or assertion I make." Argon sighed heavily. "This is *our* law, Cato. I promised her to him. I stood before his family and mine, in front of our council, and I vowed Abrial's hand to his. If I could undo that, I would, but the vow cannot be undone. Once made, the only one who can break it is Teo, and he refuses to do so. My hands are tied." The last Argon spoke slowly, drawing out each word on a wave of sorrow and apology.

"Please..." Cato bowed his head. "I'm begging. For the sake of my son, I'm begging you to help me, Argon."

"I can't." Argon shook his head. The evidence of his inner torment spilled from the depths of his bright blue eyes. What was happening to Rysk obviously upset Argon as much as it did Cato. "I would if I could, Cato. It pains me to see you and your family suffering like this, but—"

"But Rysk has *mated* Abrial." King Cato got up and paced behind his ornate chair, frustrated. "He must be allowed to be with her."

These negotiations weren't going well. Little by little, he could feel his son slipping way. He was losing, but he refused to let that happen. He didn't want to nullify the alliance between his family and Argon's, and thus end the existence of peace between the *upir* and the drecks, but Cato couldn't let his son die without a fight.

Was he really considering turning against his oldest and best friend? Argon had rallied the drecks to the *upir's* uprising against the Dacians long ago, and a long-standing camaraderie had existed ever since. Without the drecks' help, the *upir* might still be under Dacian rule, held down by Dacian oppression and cruelty.

But the *upir* were still stronger than the drecks. *Upir* blood and *upir* venom were both hardier and more powerful than that of the drecks, which meant the *upir* themselves were superior in all respects. If Cato pushed the issue, there would be no contest in taking Abrial away from Teo by force.

This was a decision Cato didn't want to make. Argon was

his friend. The drecks were *upir* allies. They had stood side by side in battle. They had shared blood and death. All to remove the Dacians from power and institute a new regime, one that was more benevolent and compassionate. And now Cato was contemplating an end to that benevolence. Shame on him. He couldn't do that. Not against his friend.

Argon stood and joined Cato by the shuttered window. He settled his hand on Cato's shoulder. "Teo refuses to budge, Cato. I'm sorry. I will try again, but I fear the cause is lost."

Teo. A dreck. The highbred son of one of Argon's upper circle. How had Teo earned the right to take what belonged to Rysk?

"Argon, you are one of my oldest friends," Cato said, lifting his head, beseeching him. "I know what I'm asking is unorthodox, but my son is in his *calling*. If he is denied, he will die. Please...you must help me. Surely, there is something that can be done."

The male *upir's* call to mate was the most powerful phenomenon within their race, and it was both valued and protected by Cato's royal council. Shortly after a male took a mate—it could be hours, days, or even weeks—he entered a phase known as the *calling*. A male's *calling* drove him into a relentless frenzy to sow his fertile seeds frequently inside his mate. It was not uncommon for a male in his *calling* to make dozens of deposits in one day, especially early on. As the days passed, the frequency to mate waned until it came to an end seven to fourteen days later. The *calling* was both bliss and agony on a male's body, and every male both dreaded and lived for it, knowing that even though he would endure extreme sexual response bordering on torture that it meant he was with his true mate and ready to create life with her. However, there was a dark side of the *calling*. If it was denied, and the male was not allowed to expend himself in his mate, mania and physical deterioration known as the *suffering* ensued.

More often than not, a male did not survive the *suffering*.

Argon squeezed Cato's shoulder, eyes compassionate. "I'm sorry, Cato. Unless Teo agrees to relinquish Abrial, I cannot interfere. Dreck laws are different from yours. I can't force *upir* law on my people or I will risk condemnation and possible forced abdication. I wish I could do more."

Cato frowned, out of options. He looked away and closed his eyes. He hated where this thoughts were taking him, but even if he didn't intend to see it through, he had to try. Perhaps just the threat would be enough to persuade Argon to make an exception and find a way to interfere with his daughter's mating to Teo.

"Even if it means war?" Cato refused to meet Argon's eyes at first, ashamed now that the words were out, exposed and hanging between them. He hated suggesting he would go to war to give Rysk Argon's daughter, but it was all he had left to bargain with. Finally, he turned and met Argon's gaze.

Argon's brow crinkled, and his face grew stern. "Certainly, you wouldn't take our two races to war over this and jeopardize our long friendship."

Cato sighed and turned away, embarrassed and defeated. "No." Quiet chagrin weighed heavily in his voice. "I wouldn't. I'm sorry for my hasty words. I'm simply...desperate."

Argon stepped toward Cato again, his robes swishing against the stone floor as he shifted from his human form into the blue-toned being he was in his natural state. He only showed himself in his blue-skinned, blue-eyed, black-haired persona to those he trusted most, and Cato knew it. "I know, my friend. This is hard on us both. I hate seeing you like this, and I think of Rysk as my own. I will talk to Teo again and do what I can, but I fear my attempt to convince him of giving up Abrial will be in vain. He is most ardent in his desire to keep my daughter."

Cato nodded. "I know, Argon, and I appreciate your kind words. I will convey your sympathies to Rysk and Jonet."

Jonet was Cato's queen, and even now, he could feel her anguish as she paced in the hall outside Rysk's chambers.

He and Argon embraced, and then Argon solemnly left the Great Room to return to his own palace. Once alone, Cato hurried out to check on his son. As he approached Rysk's quarters, a cry of agony ripped the air, and as he rounded the corner, Jonet turned to catch his eye. Her face was soaked with tears, and her hands worried in front of her. Her fingers twisted and clenched around each other. When she saw him, she stopped and silently implored him for good news, but the look on his face must have told her the situation was grim.

"No? Did Argon not agree?" she said, beside herself with agitation as she wiped tears from her cheeks.

He shook his head. "Our laws are not their laws. I can't force him to take Abrial away from Teo. And Teo refuses to cooperate."

Jonet broke down in violent sobs. "But...our son..."

As another agonized cry rent the air from Rysk's chamber, Cato wrapped his arms around his queen and closed his eyes. It looked as though they would lose their son. Unless Argon could work a miracle, it was only a matter of time until Rysk slipped away on a distressful sea of misery.

RYSK BEAT HIS FISTS AGAINST THE WALL, screamed until his lungs and throat burned, and clawed at his own skin. Without Abrial, he was lost. He needed his mate, needed her more than he'd ever needed anything. His body not only ached, it throbbed with the weight of agony so great that it crushed him. He had heard tales of *suffering* among the males of his race, but this was nothing like he'd expected. It was a hundred times worse.

Fragments of stone crumbled from the force of his fists as he continued to pummel the walls that held him prisoner. He was getting stronger. His pain made him powerful.

Turning his attention to the door, he threw himself against it. Again. And again. Not long before, he couldn't even budge it, but now, he felt a slight give. Once more, he flung himself against the barrier. With each impact, the wood gave a little more...and a little bit more...until finally, the wood splintered. Once more, he used his body as a battering ram, and the heavy wood cracked. Again and again, until...

The door exploded in a burst of splinters that showered the hallway. His parents stood several paces away, eyes wide, mouths opened in silent surprise. He hadn't time for them. Abrial was all he could think of.

Free of his prison, he raced toward the stone staircase that led to the dark courtyard, where he stopped and honed on Abrial's essence. Pursuing guards caught up to him and tried to restrain him, but he tossed them away as if they were dust. Nothing could keep him from his mate.

"Rysk!" His father called after him, rushing into the courtyard. "No! Don't!"

It was too late. Rysk was already away, sealing the fate of both races with every step as he raced into the dark forest. Faster than the wind, strengthened by his *calling*, he dodged trees, scaled the mountain separating his home from Abrial's, flashed through the fields, until he came to Premier Argon's palace moments later. Abrial remained quarantined inside. He could sense her sorrow, her suffering. She needed him, too.

Finally near his beloved, his body calmed enough for him to mist into her room, and there she was. His Abrial.

"Rysk!" She threw herself into his arms, sealed her lips over his.

Everything was right again. Everything was as it should be. "Abrial. My love. My world." He buried his nose in her hair and rained urgent kisses on her skin. His hard body pulsed to claim her. "Come with me." At last, he had what his heart and body needed, and her arousing fragrance was almost more than he could stand.

He was about to steal her out the window when the door to her chambers flew open. Teo charged in, sword in hand. "Get away from her!" His blue eyes flashed red then turned a furious blue. Clearly, he wasn't going to let Abrial go easily. This bastard wanted a fight, and Rysk was willing to give him one if it meant Abrial's hand.

Rysk bent forward, stance open, arms wide, fingers curled like claws. He bared his fangs and hissed. His dark gaze landed on the sword. Teo was dangerous. He could hurt Abrial, but in Rysk's hyperprotective state, he would die before he let Teo near her. She was his, and he would protect her.

"Teo, no!" Abrial latched onto Rysk's arms and slid behind him, inching toward the window as she tugged Rysk to go with her. "Let me go with him. Release me. I beg you. I don't love you, Teo. I never wanted to be with you."

Teo snarled, shimmered, and then shifted to blue as his eyes flashed red again. He bared his own fangs. "No. You are mine," he said to Abrial. "You were promised to *me*, and I will have you. I won't give you up to this...*heathen* creature!" He cast a disgusted, repulsed glance toward Rysk.

Rysk bristled and unleashed a warning growl. "She belongs to me, Teo. She is *my* mate. It is my *right*." He shielded Abrial, keeping her behind him.

Teo took a menacing step forward, his upper lip curled into a snarl. "And her father vowed her to me, in front of our families, in front of our council. That is *my* right. Yours is secondary to mine."

"No!" Rysk was on the verge of losing control. If they weren't allowed to escape soon, he would kill Teo. Not that he cared about Teo at the moment. Right now, his main concern was Abrial...to protect her. If that meant killing Teo, then that was what he would do.

"Yes!" Teo stormed forward, the muscles in his arms flexing as he raised his sword.

Rysk tried to push Abrial out of harm's way, but Teo moved swiftly and captured her wrist. "She is *my* mate, not yours, Rysk!" He began to pull her away.

With a roar, Rysk snapped his fangs, his sight sharpening as his eyes flashed yellow. Everyone knew not to touch a male *upir's* mate in such an aggressive way. Doing so was the best way to bring on a mated-male rage, and in an instant Rysk was on Teo. Mated aggression took hold.

Teo flung Abrial aside as he tried to defend himself, but Rysk was too powerful. He clawed, he bit, he battered Teo relentlessly, throwing him against the far, stone wall. The sword clattered to the floor, and Rysk went for it at the same time Teo did. But Teo was too slow. Rysk rolled, clutched the hilt inside his fist, flung himself to his back on the floor, and brought the sword up over him as Teo lunged forward. The blade impaled Teo, straight through his heart. After a breathless, conflicted moment of victory, Rysk tossed Teo off him and to the side, using the sword as leverage.

The sound of guards storming through the palace reached his ears as Abrial took his hand and helped him off the floor.

"We must go," she said. "Now!" Tears streaked her face, but joy that he had defeated Teo shone from her eyes.

He stole one final glance toward Teo, who lay in a puddle of blood, and then he turned, grabbed Abrial around the waist, fused his essence with hers, and projected them into a tunnel of vapor to their secret dwelling carved into the side of a mountain. A cave he had found while exploring.

As he and Abrial gave themselves over to the primal love between them, as well as to Rysk's *calling*, they remained oblivious to the aligning powers within their races. Time and again, he claimed her, and her body accepted what he gave. The beauty of new life sprang forth in her womb, and it seemed the world was theirs.

Teo's family was outraged by their son's murder. They appealed to Premier Argon for justice even as they sent war parties to find Rysk and Abrial. While Argon and Cato convened to arbitrate a solution, one of the hunting parties found the lovers and killed Rysk in a bloody battle. Beside himself with grief, Cato ceased all discussion with Premier Argon and sent an army to annihilate what he could of Teo's immediate family in revenge for his son's death, but many escaped and fled to safety, away from Cato and his army. Cato retrieved Abrial, pregnant with Rysk's unborn child, and refused to hand her over until his grandchild was born. Upset with this turn of events, Argon insisted on Abrial's return, but Cato refused until she gave birth. Abrial was grief-stricken. Her mate was gone, and their two families, who were at one time friends, were now at odds with one another to the extent that war seemed inevitable. A little over eight months later, she gave birth to Rysk's son prematurely. She named him Rysk after his father.

At first, the newborn seemed to bring peace between their families again, but the dreck population continued to pressure Argon for retribution against the *upir* for murdering over half the members of Teo's family, and eventually disavowed him as their ruler, inducting his son, Tauno, to replace him. Tauno wasn't as sympathetic to the *upir* as Argon and Abrial, and soon after Tauno's coronation, tensions escalated quickly between the drecks and the *upir*. Amid the chaos and skirmishes that followed, King Cato took custody of young Rysk and denied Abrial's unrelenting wish to see him. In her despair, she took her own life, too distraught to continue living.

All-out war erupted a month later.

And so, it was out of love, jealousy, and loss that the never-ending feud between the drecks and the *upir* began. A feud that led to more than a dozen wars and pitted the stronger *upir*—later to be known as vampires—against their former allies, the drecks, who were weaker in every respect but intellectually.

As the years passed into decades, centuries, and eventually millennia, the reason for the feud that turned into a war was forgotten by all but a few. Argon was driven into hiding, not even safe from his own son, who would have killed him out of spite for letting relations come to such a grievous state.

From his self-imposed exile, Argon followed the war as best he could as the two races of immortals battled for supremacy for a reason that never should have been. Rysk's and Abrial's love for one another—a love that should have been honored and treasured for its purity—had been desecrated into the cause for a race-wide tragedy. A tragedy that Argon shouldered the responsibility for. This was his fault, and one day he would make amends. He would find a way.

Until then, he would remain silent, bide his time, and prepare. He would watch his race struggle to survive in an ongoing war destined to forever play in the vampires' favor, broken only by periods of strained peace.

A peace eventually enforced by the vampire king's warriors, All the King's Men.

CHAPTER 1

Josie sat on the edge of the bathtub, her fingers threaded together in her lap as she checked the timer on the counter for the third time in twenty seconds. *Only forty more seconds to go.*

Her bare feet tapped quietly on the polished, marble floor as she blew out a breath she hadn't realized she was holding. She tucked her dark brown hair behind her ear as she dropped her gaze to admire yesterday's pedicure. The lady at the salon had chosen a dark purple polish when Josie told her to surprise her. It was a pretty shade. Reminded her of grape Skittles. She wiggled her toes, bit her bottom lip, and checked the timer again. Thirty-five seconds left.

She had waited until Tristan left for work before hurrying to the corner drugstore for a home pregnancy test. Okay, six pregnancy tests. A little overkill, but she wanted to be sure.

The tests were created for humans, but allegedly still worked on those like her, according to what she had heard over the years. Neither human nor vampire, Josie was somewhere in the middle. She was what Tristan and other vampires called a *davala*, an immortal who was once human but was turned by the bite of a vampire.

By the king's law, only the biological mate of a male vampire could be transformed into a *davala*, but Tristan had broken the law to turn her. He loved her, but he hadn't mated her. Not biologically speaking. The bond that linked traditional vampire mates to one another never formed between them. Tristan had never experienced a *calling* or a *suffering*, which only mated males were capable of having.

This made Josie even more doubtful that she would see anything but a negative on her pee stick.

Fifteen seconds to go. Really? For the love of God, could the seconds tick by any more slowly?

Being a *davala* hadn't stopped her periods from coming like clockwork every month. It looked like even immortal women still had to deal with their monthly visitors. So, her ovaries would produce eggs until the end of time. It was a small price to pay for becoming immortal. At least she didn't have to drink blood like Tristan.

She nervously eyed the timer.

When the date had come and gone on her calendar, and she didn't start...and another day came and went, and another, until eleven days had passed...well, she couldn't avoid the inevitable any longer. She had to know, so she had bought the tests.

Tristan had told her he would never be able to give her a child. She remembered that conversation so clearly.

"Maybe this time will work," she had said wistfully one night after they had made love and she was tucked inside the circle of his arms.

The year had been 1921, when she had still gone by the name Josephine. They had already been together two years since he'd saved her from the Spanish flu by making her his *davala*. They were more deeply in love than she had thought two people could be. To her, it didn't matter that he was a vampire. He was the kindest, most giving and compassionate man she had ever met.

"Josephine..." Tristan's voice sounded strained.

She turned to face him, but when she saw his dire expression, her heart sank and her smile faded. "What's wrong?"

He sighed and let go of her then rolled away before pulling himself out from under the blankets to sit on the edge of the bed, his face in his hands.

"Tristan?" She sat up and scooted to sit on her knees beside him. "You're scaring me." Did he not love her anymore? Did he want to leave?

"Josie..." It was the first time he'd ever called her that. "I need to tell you something. I had hoped..." Tears glistened in his eyes and emotion strangled his words. All she could do was wait, holding her breath, until he was able to continue. He coughed and cleared his throat, then tried again. "I had hoped things would be different for us, but the more time passes, and the longer we go without conceiving, the more I fear that..." Tears dropped to his cheeks, and he quickly slammed his eyes closed and rubbed his palms over his face as if trying to hide his sadness.

"Tristan, what's wrong? What are you telling me?" Fear gripped her heart as the first glimpse of the picture began to form.

He dropped his hands to his lap and sighed, lifting his sad, apologetic gaze to her. "Josie, I don't think I'll ever be able to give you children."

Her lungs emptied of air as if he had punched her. He pulled her into his arms and whispered how much he loved her. He kissed her hair, her eyelids, her lips, and her tears, all the while muttering what sounded like prayers or phrases of devotion in a language she didn't understand.

Then he told her everything about how a male vampire mated...about a male's *calling*...that since he had never technically mated her he would never have a *calling* with her...that he could never give her a child without a *calling*.

The conversation had imprinted on her mind like the death of a loved one, and really, being told that Tristan could never give her a son or daughter had been a little like the death of a child, because she had always wanted children. To be told she would forever remain childless had left a gaping hole in her soul, and she had cried a river in his arms, his tears adding to hers. The news that she would never have his child had been as painful for him to say as it had been for her to hear, and it had been clear that he had wanted a young with her as much as she had wanted to give him one.

So, here she sat, the twelfth day in, wondering if a miracle had occurred, waiting for pregnancy test number one to do its thing and give her a yay or a nay. Or was that a *yay* or a *damn*? She would find out in five seconds.

Four...

Three...

Two...

One...

Beep-beep-beep.

She took a hesitant breath, unwound her fingers, and slowly stood, her Skittle-purple toenails all but forgotten. The stick sat behind the timer, and she couldn't quite see the little square that would give her one line or two. Suddenly eager, she rushed to the sink and picked up the stick.

Two lines.

What did that mean? Was she pregnant or not? She couldn't remember. *Wait...think.* One line meant no and two meant yes. Wasn't that what the package insert had said? She thought so, but now she wasn't sure. Where was it? Where was the damn package insert? She spun then bolted from the bathroom to the kitchen, where the other five tests rested in the shopping bag on the counter. An empty box sat beside the bag, along with the instructions. She snagged the creased insert and skimmed through the tiny print as she hurried back to the bathroom. She stopped when she came to the paragraph about reading the results.

One line. Not pregnant.

Two lines. Pregnant.

She rushed back into the bathroom, grabbed the stick, and looked at it again. Definitely two lines.

Omigod! I'm pregnant.

To be sure, she ran back to the kitchen, grabbed another test that didn't require first-morning urine, ripped open the box, and practically sprinted back to the bathroom. She forced out enough pee to wet the stick, and then waited.

Same result.

She. Was. Pregnant.

The lights shone a little brighter, and the earth-toned colors of her bathroom seemed more vivid. She had thought she would never have Tristan's child, and yet, inside her, right now, was a tiny new life she and Tristan had created together. It was a miracle. A flipping miracle!

Josie shut off the bathroom light and wandered in a daze to the kitchen, where she plopped down on a bar stool at the open counter and thumbed blindly through one of Tristan's gun magazines. She wasn't looking at the pictures, though. She didn't see the pages at all. She was too caught up in the wonder of being pregnant to see much of anything.

For any female to become pregnant with a vampire's young when he hadn't had a *calling* was almost unheard of. It was so rare that, after their conversation almost a century ago, both she and Tristan had resigned themselves to the fact that if they wanted children of their own, they would have to adopt. They had even attempted the vampire's equivalent of in vitro without success. So to now be sitting here, with a little baby in the first stages of life inside her belly, was life altering. Josie was numb.

So many emotions rolled through her she couldn't distinguish one from another. Joy, fear, worry, elation, relief, wonder. How did she begin to process how she felt?

Suddenly, she burst into tears and laughter all at once. She was going to have a baby. Tristan's baby. *Thank you, God!*

TRISTAN SETTLED BEHIND HIS DESK IN HIS OFFICE, ready to start the team meeting.

"Where's Micah?" he said.

Everyone was there except Micah. As usual. Goddamn it. He thought that taking another mate would get Micah back on track, but it seemed more and more like Micah was falling back into his pre-Jackson, post-Katarina ways. And didn't that just reek of trouble. Micah had been the resident loner for centuries after the death of his first mate, Katarina, and even though Micah was the best enforcer on the team, Tristan didn't need any more problems from the guy.

"Well?" Tristan glanced around the room.

Io sighed as if he didn't give a rat's ass. Beside him, Arion shook his head. Off to the side, standing against the wall with his arms crossed and a matchstick between his lips, Trace didn't even flinch. That left Malek, Micah's oldest friend.

"Malek? Have you seen him?"

Malek shrugged. "Not since last night."

Tristan huffed and sat back, pen in hand. He needed Io to stay in and run intel, but if Micah didn't show up that meant Io would need to hit the field. They were already shorthanded and needed to add more members to the team, so he didn't need *No-Show Micah* to play his stupid shit games right now.

"Well then. We'll just wait," Tristan said, his irritation and temper rising.

"What if he doesn't show up at all?" Io said, leaning back and getting cozy in his chair.

"Then we'll wait all goddamn night!" Tristan stood and threw his pen on his desk. It bounced and flew across the room.

Trace's gaze followed it as it slid across the floor to stop in front of the door.

Tristan paced to the back of the windowless room and leaned against the wall, impatience oozing from every pore. He'd had enough of Micah. The guy was a walking time bomb who might or might not show up, depending on how he felt. He'd been like this for what seemed like forever, but now he was getting worse, and he feared they were all on a countdown to implosion. He knew Micah and Jackson had been arguing a lot, but this was expected since Micah had formed a mating bond to Jackson and Jackson hadn't bonded back. Now it looked like things were about to come to a head.

Ten minutes passed by the time Micah finally graced them with his presence. He stopped when he saw the pen on the floor, cracked a bemused grin, bent down, picked it up, and set it on Tristan's desk, taking his seat as if nothing were wrong.

"Nice of you to join us," Tristan said.

"No problem." Micah met his gaze with ice in his dark blue eyes.

"Selfish prick," Arion grumbled beside him. "Get your shit toge—"

Micah cut him off with a fist to the face. "Fuck off, Ari."

The room exploded with male vampire aggression, which made human testosterone outbursts look like kittens compared to lions. Io tore out of his seat and shoved Ari aside to take a swing at Micah, who kicked his chair over as he blocked Io's fist and shoved him back. Trace leaped into the fray and grabbed Micah by the shoulders to pull him away before he could turn Io's face into hamburger. Malek jumped between them, arms extended both ways as buffers.

"Enough of this shit!" Tristan pounded his fist on his desk. "Sit!" He shot daggers at both Io and Micah, but especially at Micah. "Ari! Io! Nix the editorial commentary. Micah, calm the fuck down. You *are* being a selfish prick. We've been waiting for fifteen goddamn minutes on your late ass. Don't you think we'd rather be out doing our jobs?"

Micah glared over his shoulder at Trace and flung himself out of his grasp. "Don't touch me."

Trace held his hands up as if to indicate he wasn't a threat, and then backed away.

Micah then turned on Tristan. "You don't need me here holding your hand to run your goddamn team meeting."

"You're part of the team, Micah," Tristan said. "At least for now."

Micah scoffed. "Yeah, go ahead. Kick me out. That'll be just fucking perfect."

"I don't want to kick you out, Micah, but you're starting to make me think I've got no choice."

"Whatever. You don't have the balls."

"Micah, just sit your ass down and shut the fuck up." Tristan had to have the most dysfunctional team in all of AKM's history, and Micah was a huge reason why. When Micah entered the room, tensions spiked so high it felt like mousetraps were set an inch apart around the floor. When one went off, it started a chain reaction until chaos ensued, as tonight's outburst proved. This had been just one in a long line of Micah-fueled eruptions to take place over the past few months. Then again, this was what happened when you pulled together six alpha vampires carrying enough emotional baggage to cause even the Buddha to have a nervous breakdown.

Once everyone had settled back down, Tristan took a deep breath and gave the quick and dirty, sixty-second version of tonight's meeting, then dismissed everyone but Micah.

"I can't take much more of this insubordination, Micah," Tristan said when they were alone. "You're my best enforcer, but you're a live wire right now. What's going on with you and Jackson? Is everything all right?" Theirs was such a complicated relationship that nobody—and not even Micah from the looks of it—could fully understand or make sense of it.

Micah huffed out a derisive puff of breath and looked away. "Who are you? Dr. Phil?"

"Micah—"

"Look, I'm here. Isn't that enough? So get off my ass." He stood, marched to the door, flung it open, and with a last glare over his shoulder, stormed out.

Damn. Micah and Jackson had clearly argued again. Tristan had a bad feeling about this. If Micah lost another mate—if that's what Jackson really was, because they didn't have a normal mated relationship—a body bag wouldn't be far behind. Maybe a bunch of body bags. He remembered how Micah was after losing Katarina. Lost, violent, a threat to himself and others. It had taken decades for Micah to recover enough from Katarina's death to be able to function even halfway like his old self.

Jackson had given Micah new life, new happiness. But all that would crumble to shit if Jackson took off on him. And then who knew how far Micah would fall? Pretty damn far if history was any indication.

Tristan hung his head. He didn't want to lose his friend again, because this time, the loss might well be permanent. Tristan might end up being the one to implant the bullet in Micah's temple, but that was the reality of his job. Sometimes hard decisions had to be made to save the greater population from harm. And if Micah lost Jackson, he would become the greatest kind of harm their kind had ever seen.

CHAPTER 2

KING BAIN FINGERED THE MEDALLION that hung around his neck as he scanned the archives that had been passed down from his father. The medallion, which was his family's royal crest, had been in his bloodline since his ancestor, Cato, claimed the throne after ousting the barbaric Dacian clan from rule. Made from bronze, the medallion was embellished with ancient glyphs and displayed two swords crossed over a full moon. He wore the round amulet whenever he met with dignitaries, oversaw proceedings in his court, or otherwise conducted royal business.

Today he was meeting with Premier Royce, the leader of the drecks and a descendant of Argon, who the lore spoke of as being a onetime ally with King Cato. Bain struggled to believe that his forefather had ever been friends with the drecks, but who was he to dispute the archives, which held more than a few surprises within their pages. He brushed his fingertips over his family tree, which was included in the royal book of records he kept secured on a marble pedestal in his study. He eyed the names of his ancestors and extended family, feeling an ache over the secrets they held, but which he was not at liberty to reveal until the time was right, if it ever would be.

With a sigh, he gently closed the tome, placed the Plexiglas cover back on the pedestal, locked the case, and turned his thoughts back to Royce.

According to history, their two families had once been allies. Even close friends. That had been a long time ago, though. Bain was six generations removed from King Cato, while Premier Royce was the ninth generation of Argon's line. Cato and Argon had been in power when the first war broke out between their races, and Bain had learned the whole sordid history—at least as much as had been preserved in the archives—soon after coming into power after his father's death in the Middle Ages. And what a tragic, ugly history it was, if the recorded lore was true.

Bain closed his eyes. That wasn't the only hard truth he had to bear from the royal archives, but he feared the time would never come for him to reveal the rest, especially where his mentor, Micah Black, was concerned. Micah had trained him when he was a child, and he was the mightiest warrior Bain had ever known. But Micah had been lost to mated *suffering* for a millennium. Until he came back to his senses, his rightful place—which Bain's father, Bain the First, had always hoped to see realized—would have to remain a secret.

"Premier Royce has arrived and is waiting for you."

Bain turned to find his secretary waiting just inside the door of his office. "Thank you." He adjusted his tailored suit—because, for one, the king didn't buy off-the-rack, and for another, it was hard to find clothes to fit a seven-foot-tall behemoth built like a linebacker—and followed his secretary down the hall to his conference center.

"Premier Royce, always a pleasure," he said, hand outstretched. If what the archives said was true, Bain imagined that their ancestors never had to fake such pleasant salutations.

"Likewise, King Bain. You look well." Royce shook his hand as he shifted to blue. "You don't mind…?"

Bain waved him off. "Of course not. Make yourself comfortable."

In their natural state, drecks appeared blue. Blue skin, blue eyes, blue nails. Even their hair was bluish-black. In their dreck state, they wore their hair long, and their faces appeared more elongated. Some might describe their features as gaunt, or perhaps taut. Drecks preferred to remain hidden in human form, though, and could shift into any persona they liked, although once they chose a human image, they usually stuck with it.

"How's Queen Cara?" Royce said as he took a glass of wine offered by Bain's secretary.

Bain always kept a stash of aged red wine on hand for Royce, who had a taste for it.

"She's well," Bain said, selecting water instead. "And how is Lady Jora?"

Royce nodded as he sipped his wine. "Better than ever." He regarded the glass. "Delicious, as always," he said. "I do so enjoy our meetings a little bit more because you serve me such rare vintages."

Bain gestured toward a seat. "I'm nothing if not hospitable. Please, have a seat."

He and Royce met once every month to keep an open line of communication between their races, but Bain felt their meetings were little more than a front. Especially as of late. His instincts told him Royce was hiding something.

"Have you made any headway on finding the source of cobalt manufacturing or distribution?" Bain said after a few more pleasantries and small talk.

Cobalt had first appeared in the 1980s as a human recreational drug, but had quickly found its way into the vampire population for its ability to provide an intense high that vampires couldn't get from other human drugs. Not even alcohol could keep a vampire drunk for long, and hangovers lasted all of an hour in all but the most extreme cases. For vampires who longed for a dip into the wild side, cobalt provided the right avenue of self-destruction, and while the dreck-made drug had remained small-time for the better part of the three decades since it was first introduced, the last year had seen an incredible surge in use. Almost as if vampires were purposely being sought in droves by cobalt dealers.

God forbid if cobalt ever found its way into the royal family. Bain didn't think he would be able to deal with that. Certainly his son and daughter would have the sense not to degrade the family name that way. He had an image to protect—a picture of control and power he had to keep in place for his people. He couldn't afford to be seen as weak or to have the royal line tainted with such corruption.

"No, not yet," Royce said. "My people are still following up on leads."

"Your people have been following up on leads for months, Royce. Meanwhile, my people are dying."

Cobalt overdose was becoming more prolific. And overdoses ended in death in almost half the cases. His enforcement agency, All the King's Men, had been hauling in dealers for months, but it seemed like for every one they brought in, two more took his place. Vampire Dreck Affairs in Atlanta had raided a manufacturing facility going on a year ago that had been a bloodbath. Those drecks had been well funded and heavily armed, and many agents and enforcers had been killed. Still, for all their raids and arrests, they were no closer to having answers than they had been a year ago. The vampire community wasn't in an epidemic—at least, not yet. However, if they didn't get answers soon, it was hard telling how bad the situation could get.

Royce sighed sympathetically. "I know, Bain, and I'm truly sorry. We're doing all we can, but whoever is making and distributing cobalt has done a good job to hide their tracks."

Bain's eyes narrowed. He wished he could see inside Royce's mind, but part of their truce was that he wouldn't dig inside his thoughts during their meetings. If he did, Royce would feel him. Bain couldn't hide the niggling, worming sensation those being probed felt. The only beings vampires could go mind running in without being detected were humans. Of course, there were exceptions, but more often than not, that was the rule.

If only Micah were here. Micah was the only vampire Bain knew who was capable of thought patrol without being detected. Micah heard everything in every mind in a room without even trying. How he shut that shit off so he didn't go crazy was a mystery, but it sure was a nice gift to have at times like this, when Bain wanted desperately to probe Royce's private thoughts for signs of betrayal.

"What strides have you made?" Royce asked. "Have your

enforcers turned up anything?"

Bain shook his head. "They arrest dealers almost every night, but so far my men have turned up only dead ends. And since we're not allowed to hold them for more than a few days..." He eyed Royce and shrugged, making it clear he needed Royce to reconsider the terms of the truce.

All the King's Men had been created after the last war between their races to uphold the truce and maintain the peace. Since vampires were inherently stronger than drecks, Bain had made it a stipulation of the peace negotiations that an enforcement agency would be created, and that drecks caught breaking the law or engaging in potentially aggressive behavior, or behavior that could lead to a violation of the truce, would be arrested and contained within the king's agency. Royce, who had just taken power of the drecks after his predecessor was killed, agreed to the AKM agency on one condition. That any drecks arrested could not be contained for more than thirty days—and thirty days was only for the most heinous acts—and would be turned over to the drecks for prosecution.

The deal had been a hollow victory, but one Bain could digest with the knowledge that his warriors would be the primary peacekeepers between the two races.

Unfortunately, drug dealing wasn't considered a heinous act, and he was forced to turn the dealers he caught over to the drecks within a week of arresting them. And since dreck laws were more lenient than vampire laws, they had started to see repeat offenders. A lot of them. The same dealers being arrested two or even three times in less than a year.

"Perhaps we need to revisit incarceration and punishment for dealers," Bain said, watching Royce's reaction closely.

"What do you mean?"

Bain told him of the repeat arrests. "Obviously, your punishments aren't getting the job done, Royce. The same drecks are being arrested time and again. Perhaps you're allowing these criminals to be released too quickly." All this diplomatic beating around the bush made Bain's skin crawl.

Royce smiled, but the polite display looked forced. "You

handle vampire affairs your way, Bain, and I'll handle dreck affairs mine."

"No offense," Bain held his hands up as if to convey he wasn't trying to step on toes. These political dances with Royce could be so sensitive. He had to tiptoe and dance around hot topics as if he were Fred Astaire.

"None taken." Royce's false smile smoothed into a placated grin.

"I'm only suggesting that if we're going to work together to catch whoever's manufacturing cobalt, as we've agreed, that more cooperation surrounding the length of incarceration of dealers could be beneficial." More tap dancing.

"Noted," Royce said dismissively. "I'll consider it." He paused. "Now, I'd like to talk about the excessive force one of your enforcers used to take down a dreck who stole a human female's purse."

It looked like the cobalt discussion was tabled. For now. Bain would continue pushing the topic in future meetings, and if Royce continued to give him the same mealy-mouthed answers and noncommittal horseshit much longer, he would take matters into his own hands, even if it meant risking peace. He put on a steely smile as his head began to ache. This was going to be a long night.

CHAPTER 3

TRISTAN UNLOCKED THE DOOR TO HIS SUITE at AKM where he spent most of his time with Josie. Several members of AKM stayed at the facility at least part of the time, mostly team leaders and medical personnel who had to remain on call. Basically, anyone who needed to be able to respond quickly when an emergency arose had a housing unit on site.

He smiled at the candles on the table and the scent of homemade Italian food, which Josie loved cooking for him on special occasions. When he had called earlier to tell her he would be late, she had said she had something to tell him, and now he wondered what the good news was. If she'd made Italian and pulled out the candles, she was obviously excited about something. Maybe she had finally been accepted to the nursing program at AKM. She volunteered in the medical ward occasionally, but despite completing the vampire equivalent of nursing school six months ago, there had been a waiting list for an internship. Maybe she had finally received the call.

After setting his duffel in the chair near the door, he followed her floral scent to the bedroom, where he found her curled on her side, hugging his pillow against her body. She was asleep, but dressed in what looked like a new negligee, and her dark brown hair spilled in thick waves over her face and against the white pillowcase.

His body reacted, growing hard. For all intents and purposes, Josie was his mate. The one and only female he would ever love. Just because his biological forces hadn't fired up to stake a mated claim on her like that of other mated pairs, she still belonged to him, and he to her. He had chosen her even if his body hadn't formed the invisible link necessary for the king's law to officially recognize her as his legal mate. Even so, he and everyone else referred to as such.

She looked like a goddess in her dark red nighty. Red was such a beautiful color on her, with her dark hair and tan skin.

He pulled his long-sleeved sweater and T-shirt over his head, and then joined her in bed.

"Baby, I'm home." He scooted up behind her and skimmed his fingertips down her slender arm as he pressed his lips against the back of her shoulder.

She stirred and quietly squeaked deep in her throat as she stretched against him. "Hey," she said sleepily, turning her head.

He brushed her hair out of her face. "Hey, sleepyhead."

She grinned. "I was tired."

"You've been tired a lot lately. You okay?"

Her grin spread into a straight-toothed smile. "I'm perfect." She turned in his arms, wrapped hers around his shoulders, and combed her fingers through his hair.

"Perfect, huh?" He tipped her face to his and brushed his lips over hers.

She nodded, coquettish and gorgeous, her light brown, green-and-gold-flecked eyes sparkling.

"How about you share some of your perfection with me then." He winked and slid the negligee up her hips. She wore a lacy thong underneath, and he squeezed one perfect orb of flesh on her bottom as he rolled to his back and pulled her on top of him.

"Rough night?" Her fingers made short work of the fastenings on his pants, and he helped her push them down his thighs.

"Not anymore." Together, they managed to get his pants and boxers into a bundle at the foot of the bed. "Now that I'm in your capable hands." He moaned and closed his eyes as her palm wrapped around his erection.

"My capable hands?" Amused arousal tinged her voice.

"Oh, baby, you have no idea how unbelievably capable

your hand is right now."

She giggled and nibbled the side of his neck with butterfly bites and nectar kisses as he snagged the bit of floss on her rump and snapped it without so much as an ounce of effort.

Her sigh told him she approved.

No matter how bad his nights were, or how much Micah got on his nerves, he could always come home to Josie, and she made everything all right. She was the calm he needed to unwind, the breath he needed to relax, the breeze to whisper his soul into submission. Josie was what every male searched for in a mate. She was his ideal, his match, his perfect complement.

"I'm grateful for the day I found you, baby," he whispered into her hair.

"Me, too." Her nimble hand gently rode up his shaft, then back down.

He groaned and tipped his head back as her mouth slid down to his Adam's apple. Her tongue swirled firm circles around and around, and still farther down to the hollow between his collarbones. All the while, her hand worked magic on him.

"You always know what I need," he said.

She rose up his body and licked his lips. "That's because I'm so unbelievably in love with you."

"Even after all this time."

"*Especially* after all this time."

Not only did she know what to do, she knew what to say. Tristan wasn't fooling himself. He knew that since they hadn't technically mated one another that their relationship could slip away. Another could come along and mate her, or he could mate another, and then their relationship would be null, no matter how long they had been together. And it wasn't just the threat of another mate coming along. Like humans, without the biological link to bind them to one another, he and Josie could simply fall out of love at some point. Grow tired of one another and lose the magic they'd managed to cultivate for nearly a hundred years. But for now, that wasn't happening. They were together, in love, and devoted to one another.

"I love you," he said.

"Duh," she answered with a coy wink.

"Hey now, no need to get sassy." He swatted her bottom and grabbed the back of her thigh—where she was wickedly ticklish—with his other hand and squeezed.

She threw her head back in a fit of giggles, squirming as he wriggled his fingers against her flesh. "Stop! Oh my God. Tristan!" She squealed and writhed against him, which stoked his arousal even more.

Laughing but on fire to give himself to her, he flipped her to her stomach and shifted to pin her down as he shoved up the nighty to reveal her perfect ass, smooth and round and out of this world sexy.

"Tristan!" She gasped as he bent and playfully bit her right cheek and held her down with his hands gripping either side of her hips.

She liked when he played with her ass, which was perfect since he liked playing with it. Her bottom was firm and round, the ideal derriere for an ass man like Tristan. At least Mother Nature had gotten that part of their relationship right. It would have sucked if Josie didn't get so worked up with butt play. As it was, her bottom was the surest way to rev her engine. She loved when he spanked her, loved when he pinched her cheeks, bit them, or slid his fingers down the crease as he was now. In an instant, she was breathing heavily into the comforter, her fingers fisting handfuls of fabric at her sides.

That was his Josie, his sexy freak in bed.

He lay down on her back, reached into the nightstand, and pulled out the body oil as he nibbled the back of her shoulder. Then he rose to his knees between her legs and drizzled her backside with a generous dose of slippery wetness before pouring some into his palm.

"You're in a mood tonight, baby," he said, stroking oil over his erection with one hand as he massaged her left cheek with the other.

Her shoulders hunched as she drew her arms in and

squirmed, moving her ass side to side as if trying to encourage his hand to explore her everywhere. "Uh-huh," she managed to breathe out. She bent her right leg, and her heel playfully bumped the back of his arm.

"What's got you so hot? Huh, baby?" Tristan squeezed both hands around her luscious cheeks and slid his cock smoothly between them as he pushed on the sides to close her flesh around him. The friction was delicious, and beneath him, she moaned and panted desperately as he drove his cock forward and back, forward and back, groaning at the sight of his head poking out from between her oil-slicked cheeks with every upward thrust.

He shifted his knees to push her legs wider and leaned over her, arms planted on either side of her torso so he could glide his cock up and down the slippery cleft of her ass, and then all the way up the center of her back, which glistened with oil. Slowly, he made love to her back, trailing the length of his cock up and down and across her skin, using his erection like a brush to spread the oil all over her. The slick sensation of gliding against her skin and back down to her ass drove him wild, and Josie seemed to be just as keyed up as he was. Maybe even more so. Lusty, make-me-come moans broke from her throat with every breath, and her long fingers twisted and kneaded the blankets into vicious mounds.

Easing himself down on her back, he drove his cock into the part of her ass again. "What's got you so hot for me tonight, baby?"

She simply mewled in reply, as if begging him not to stop.

"You want me here?" He pressed more firmly between her cheeks, right where he knew she wanted him.

Josie enjoyed anal sex, which no one would have guessed from looking at her. She appeared so straight and laced up, but in the bedroom, she turned into a vixen. She was the epitome of a lady in the street but a freak in the bed, so it was no surprise that she arched her back and lifted her ass against him, silently begging him not to stop.

She nodded urgently as she shot him a salacious, over-the-shoulder glance that bitch-slapped his inner hedonist so hard his cock wept. "Yes. Please yes." She practically moaned the words.

With the temperature rising and no time to lose, he grabbed the bottle of oil, lifted himself, doused the crease of her bottom again, then tossed the bottle aside and eased back down, letting his hard-on collect plenty of lubricant as it glided toward home.

Her hands clenched the sheets, and her body shuddered as the head gained entry. Sweet bliss. So snug. So damn sexy. Josie lifted her hips, wordlessly begging him for more as she whimpered and clawed the bedding.

No matter how often he took her this way, he always started slowly. They both loved feeling him glide in and out of her, and watching his cock disappear little by little nearly drove him delirious with lust. Besides, he could thrust—and would—once the lube made the way easier.

Applying gentle pressure, he eased inside a little at a time, pulled back slightly, pushed forward, glided back out, slid deeper, until finally he was all the way. He grunted as he lay down over her back and flexed his hips, grinding against her as he drove himself deep. She gasped and reached for his hand.

He wound his fingers around hers and, together, they fisted the comforter as they found their rhythm. One that came from decades of experience. A rhythm that flowed through them as naturally as blood. After so long together, he knew her body, and she knew his. He knew what she wanted by the way she moaned. Whether or not she wanted it fast or slow by the tension in her fingers, and how close she was to coming by the quick, shallow, punctuated gasps that came seconds before she ruptured.

And right now she wanted it hard and fast. She was on fire tonight.

"God, baby, you're like an animal."

She grunted and flung her head back against his shoulder. "More."

And he gave her more. So much more. Josie spurred him to

reach heights he hadn't found during sex in months. God, he loved this side of her, and he held on tight as he pumped his hips in rapid thrusts, drawing urgent cries and demanding commands of "harder, faster" from her.

Sweat poured from his scalp, down his back, and over his chest, mixing with the oil to create the most unreal, erotic slickness between their bodies. His thick biceps clenched, his legs stiffened and shook, and beneath him, Josie entered the point of no return. Her gasps tightened, grew shallow, and her body quieted as she seemed to hold her breath.

She was going to come. And so was he. So close. They were going to crash together. What a fucking rush.

"Baby, baby...yes..." He slammed his eyes shut, ground his teeth, and felt her approaching orgasm rise as if on a geyser.

And then the geyser gave and the world crashed around them.

Her cries mingled with his, and he thrust hard, once, twice, three times—each involuntary, ass-clenching contraction like an exclamation point—as he spilled inside her, grunting his pleasure until he finally collapsed on her back.

Josie completed his life. She was his mate now and forever, in every way except one, but at times like this, that didn't matter. They were so perfectly in tune with one another that Tristan had begun to think that not even a biological bond could be stronger.

"That was a nice welcome home," he said moments later, breathless. He tucked his face against the side of her neck. A final pulse of orgasm tightened his body, and he moaned as every muscle clenched, and then he sighed as he molded into her.

He felt her cheek lift against his face and knew she was smiling.

"Unexpected," she said softly.

"Very." He eased out of her and rolled to the side and propped himself on one elbow, letting the fingers of his other hand skim the supple, oil-smoothed skin of her back and shoulders. "Have I told you lately how beautiful you are?"

She lifted to her elbows and turned smoky eyes on him.

"I think you might have mentioned it last night, before you left for work." She leaned toward him and kissed him softly, sweetly.

"Mm." He nodded introspectively and grinned. "I guess I did. But I'll say it again. You're beautiful."

"So are you." She shifted to her side to face him and rumpled his hair. "But you need a haircut, handsome."

He raked his fingers through his hair and tousled it. "What? You don't like the mangy grunge look I'm going for?" He sat up and turned so he could look in the mirror. His blond hair stuck out in every direction.

Josie pushed herself up and pressed behind him, arms around his chest, legs circling his hips, and rested her cheek against the center of his back. "You wear mangy grunge well, baby."

Her fingers caressed his stomach, and he placed his hands over hers. "You wear *everything* well." He looked over his shoulder as she lifted her face from his back and met his gaze. They kissed, holding their intimate caress for several long, luxurious moments before Tristan broke away. "So, what's the good news?"

Josie's eyes lit, and her face brightened. And were those tears? She must have really wanted that internship. He had no idea it was that important to her.

"Oh, Tristan..." For a heartbeat, her eyes searched his, gleaming with moisture, and then she blinked rapidly and looked away.

Tristan turned and cradled her face in his hands. "Baby? What is it?"

Their eyes met again, and the smile that spread over her face could only be described as joyous, if not slightly angelic, because that's just how Josie looked. Like an angel. His angel. He'd always thought so.

"Tristan," she said, "I'm pregnant."

At first, he wasn't sure he'd heard her right. Pregnant? How could she be pregnant? He hadn't had a *calling*. He had never had a *calling*. So wasn't it impossible for her to be pregnant? Obviously he had misheard her, but the expectant, heartwarming expression on her face said otherwise.

"But...how?" His brain resisted accepting the news, even though he desperately wanted to believe it.

Josie's soft, giddy laughter tickled his ears. "I don't know, Tristan, but I'm pregnant."

"But I haven't had a *calling*," he said quietly, dismayed. "How—?" He blinked rapidly, eyes flitting blindly around the room as if he were searching for a more logical explanation.

"I know, but"—Josie leaped out of bed and rushed to the bathroom. When she returned, she held two white sticks. Pregnancy tests. She shoved them in front of him. "Look!"

Tristan gingerly plucked the plastic sticks from her fingers and stared at them, stunned. "I don't know what I'm looking for." Two pink lines in a small window stared back at him from one, and a blue plus sign was displayed on the other. Okay, so he got the second one. Positive. But the first...?

Josie pointed. "Two lines means pregnant." Then she pointed to the other one. "This one...well, it's a plus sign, which means positive."

Tristan had resigned himself a long time ago to the idea that he and Josie would never have children, but in his hands, he now held evidence to the contrary.

When he lifted his gaze to hers, she beamed. Literally beamed as if she'd never been so happy. More than likely, she had gone through the same disbelief and denial he was going through now when she viewed her test results earlier, but after the realization finally sunk in, to learn she was pregnant had probably sent her to the moon.

For a heartbeat, Tristan held his breath and searched her eyes for any hesitance, and then he couldn't wait any longer. He had to know for himself. He couldn't rely on these human tests to tell him what he could prove with his own hands. In a rush of excitement, he dropped the two white sticks on the bed and planted one palm against her lower belly as he pulled her closer with his other arm. He might not have had his *calling*, but that didn't mean he wouldn't be able to feel the energy of a tiny, new life growing inside Josie's womb.

Closing his eyes, he concentrated on Josie's breath, wound

his essence inside her energy, felt her heartbeat, and dove deeper. From within Josie's life signature, another much smaller one emerged. A tiny ball of tightly bound energy swirled within her, distinct and separate, but still a part of her. And he felt his own signature mingled within the new. His child. That was his unborn son or daughter inside Josie's belly.

"Well?" Josie clutched his shoulders.

Opening his eyes, he met her gaze. Tears burned and pooled on his lower lids. "So this is why you've been so tired lately." Dumbfounded, he began putting the pieces together. Josie had been unusually tired for over a week, and her breasts were tender. She had complained of that almost two weeks ago. He blinked, and tears dropped to his cheeks.

"Can you feel it?" She placed her hand over his, and hope sprang from her touch. "Can you feel our baby?" she said quietly, as if she didn't want to breathe for fear he would tell her she had been mistaken...that the pregnancy tests had given a false positive.

He nodded, his emotions forming a brutal lump in his throat. He had always wanted this. Against all hope, he had always yearned for a child with Josie. "Yes."

She burst into tears, threw her arms around his head, and hugged his face to her chest.

Tristan mashed her body to his and held her tightly as emotions he didn't know he'd been holding for decades gushed from him in heavy sobs. He was going to be a father.

CHAPTER 4

MICAH KNELT ON THE ROOF OF HIS APARTMENT BUILDING in downtown Chicago and overlooked the city. Christmas lights blinked from windows, from trees along the street, and in the parks visible from his vantage point. It was a season of joy, but not for Micah. Joy wasn't meant for him, anymore. It hadn't been for a long time.

Dawn was less than an hour from breaking, but he had no desire to escape to the safety and warmth of his apartment on the eighteenth floor. Jackson wasn't there, so all that waited for him was loneliness and silence.

How had he formed a bond to Jackson when the guy hadn't formed a bond back? This wasn't how mating worked, if what he had with Jackson could even be called a mating. Case in point, he had never had a *calling* with Jackson, at least not a "normal" one. Sure, he'd said he did, and he *had* been all over Jackson those first few days, but what he had felt had been nothing like what he'd felt with Katarina. But it wasn't just that. His feelings for Jackson felt misdirected in some way, as if they had been meant for someone else. If that was the case, then why had they manifested with Jackson? Still, he knew what he knew, and for all intents and purposes, he was a mated male. Maybe in his own way, but whether for right or wrong, normal or not, he had mated Jackson.

But then Micah was an enigma...a fucking anomaly. Nothing about him was right or normal. He was cursed with misfortune and pain. Always had been, always would be. Nothing about him was the way it "should" be or the way it was for other vampires, but he had learned to deal with his odd divergence centuries ago. Jackson not requiting the bond between them was just one more piece of proof of how different he was.

He had found requited love once. Nearly a thousand years ago he had mated Katarina. Beautiful, raven-haired Katarina. He had loved her from youth, smitten with her practically from the moment he could walk. Micah had known from a young age he would mate her when he transitioned, and just as he had preordained, after he returned home from the war, he did just that. She had been at the celebration for his return, and the moment he saw her, the mating link began to form.

Their love had been magical, despite the fact she couldn't have children. Not many female vampires were infertile, but she was. After his *calling*, when he checked her womb for life, nothing stirred within. They had both been devastated, because they'd been eager for a family, but Micah didn't let their inability to have children hold him down for long. He was grateful to have Katarina at all, and nothing would lessen his love for her.

Then she was killed in a raid. Not even two years after they had mated, she was gone.

Micah bit back the sting of tears as he remembered the day she had been taken from him. How he had held her in his arms as she breathed her last breath. How he had begged her not to go, not to leave him. How he had professed his undying love for her as she slipped away.

"Please don't leave me," he had said. He could remember it like it was yesterday. "I love you. You can't die, Kat. I waited so long for you. I came back for you. For *you*." Tears streamed his dirty, blood-covered cheeks. "Please." He scrunched his eyes closed, forcing his unshed tears to fall so he could see her clearly, not through the gauzy vision impaired by his tears.

"Micah…" She could barely speak, barely move, but managed to lift her hand to his face. "Be…strong." She blinked heavily. "Survive."

"No. Not without you." He clutched her close, rocked her, tried to breathe life into her, but it was too late. He had seen enough death and battle wounds to know Kat wouldn't survive hers. He had only seconds left with her.

"Micah. Promise me." She fought for breath. "You promise me now...that you will survive. Don't..." She began to fade in and out. "Don't...let me die...without your promise. Honor me...by living."

What could he do? This was his love, his life, his precious mate. And she wanted him to promise her he would live even though she—his reason for living—was about to die?

"Pro...mise...me." Her hold on his hand weakened.

Cursing God, Micah bowed his head and fought back a sob. If this was what she needed to die peacefully, he would give it to her. He would give anything to Katarina, even his life if God had been merciful enough to take him instead.

"I promise," he said. "I promise you. For you, I'll do anything, my love." He kissed her forehead, her nose, her lips.

A faint smile touched her mouth. "I...love...you...Micah."

"I love you." He tipped his forehead to hers and held her fading gaze. "I will always love you. Forever."

A few seconds later, the life had left her, and the light that had been Katarina vanished from Micah's life in a blink, without fanfare, and for eternity. A casualty of the ongoing war with the drecks, she had joined half of Micah's village in death.

Micah blinked against Chicago's lights. Why couldn't he have died, too? Life had been so perfect with her. With Katarina, he had been a true male, whole and complete. Not even her inability to have young had dampened his power and sense of worth. But now, all that was gone.

Micah bowed his head, and his long, black hair lifted on the stinging December wind that blew off Lake Michigan. He slowly wiped the pad of his thumb under one eye, then the other, brushing away his bitter tears.

After Kat's death, he had fallen. To shame. To disgrace. Into the depths of hell. His degradation had known no bounds.

In the moment of her death, he had vowed retribution, but first came the *suffering* of loss. The need to hurt himself, and the desire to die. Without Kat, his soul fractured. Not even

Malek, who had been his best friend at the time—so close they were more like brothers—could get through to him.

Only by force of will and his promise to Kat did he survive months of *suffering*, but that didn't mean he became his old self again when the *suffering* ended. On the contrary, he was a hollowed shell, flesh and bone without a soul, the worst version of himself. That's when he hunted down the drecks who had killed her and murdered every last one. The hunt lasted for over a century and earned him a reputation with both drecks and vampires as being the most ruthless, deadliest warrior in the king's army. Except Micah had left the king's army to fulfill his personal vendetta. What he had done, he did outside the realm of the king's command.

Then the women came. And the men.

He didn't think of himself as bisexual, which was a label for humans. That meant nothing to him. Many vampires who had lived without a mate for as long as he had often scratched their curious itch when it came to same-sex relationships. And for vampires as old as he was, lying with a male was as normal as lying with a female, although Micah preferred the latter. But back then, when he had been strangled by misery's hand, he hadn't been choosy. He had simply needed companionship. A warm body to press against in the night. A tender expanse of skin to sink his fangs into and feed from as he had once fed from his beloved Katarina.

Disgraced and disgusted with himself, he had roamed and wandered like a gypsy for centuries, lost to all he had once known, as likely to kill as he was to save. For a while, his discretion severely lacked, and he wasn't proud of some of the things he had done during that tumultuous time in his life.

Slowly, he began to find himself again, and wound his way back to the King's Guard. Tristan and Malek greeted him warmly enough, but in their eyes Micah saw the realization that he had changed. They were hesitant to embrace him as they once had, and he couldn't blame them. He was no longer the male he once was, but at least he was alive. At least he had kept his promise to Kat and lived.

Silent and brooding more often than not, he found that much had changed. Bain the First had been assassinated, and Bain the Second had risen to power. Many things had stayed the same, though. Vampires were still at war with the drecks, and the fighting saved Micah from delirium.

In battle, he was a force of nature. Fierce, relentless, almost savage, and always heartless. Micah fought with no regard for his own life, as if every battle would be his last, and he had vowed to take as many as he could with him before he died. He reasoned that if he died in battle, he wouldn't really be breaking his promise to Kat, but somehow he always managed to survive. Over time, his reputation for being the most ruthless warrior in the King's Guard intensified. He became the most feared of all King Bain's warriors. And when King Bain created All the King's Men, Micah's reputation followed him. He was the one enforcer no dreck wanted to come up against, because he pushed the boundaries of the truce to their limits, and maybe even crossed them once or twice. He was an unleashed rabid dog.

Unfortunately, not even his reputation and his dominant demeanor could pull him from the devil's grasp. He had never recovered from Kat's death, and his *suffering* followed him everywhere.

However, in 1975, he discovered bondage. He found he liked the power exchange between a Dom and sub, as well as the trust between partners and—for a little while at least—BDSM became a means to channel his pain and to feel a sense of worth again. His submissives cut through to engage that inner part of him that desperately wanted to care for another the way he had Katarina, and within months, he was fully immersed in the leather lifestyle.

Bondage play, S&M, and other aspects of BDSM gave him focus, and he studied with the best Doms, both human and vampire alike, to master every aspect of the trade. His teammates at AKM didn't understand his immersion into leather, but for him, taking a sub to the very limits, shattering her—or him—then bringing her back from the brink into wholeness became therapeutic. He relished the after care, where he held his sub, soothed her, tended to any wounds he inflicted, and escaped into his own endorphin high.

But as with everything else in his life, bondage and S&M began to lose its appeal in the mid-90s after he caused tremendous mental and physical trauma to a relatively new sub during fire play. Through all their communication up front about what was and wasn't acceptable, the sub had never told him fire play was a hard limit or that his sister had died in a house fire when they were kids. Even though Micah could dip inside people's minds at will without even trying—another piece of evidence to how much of a freak he was—he hadn't seen the memory of the sub's sister in his thoughts until the moment he lit his cheesecloth-tipped wand. The sub freaked and thrashed, and suddenly Micah's mind was filled with the sub's terror. By then, it was too late. The sub's arms had been bound, but not his legs, and he ended up knocking the jar of alcohol over, getting some on him, and into an open flame. The sub's leg lit up like a torch. Micah could still hear his terrified, tortured screams.

Fortunately, Micah always kept emergency supplies nearby, and he doused the fire within seconds, but not before the alcohol vapor burned off and the sub's skin was burned badly enough to blister.

After that, Micah lost his love of BDSM. Well, more like he lost trust in himself to perform without hurting anyone, despite twenty solid years as a much sought after Master-turned-Lord. He had remained out of the lifestyle ever since.

Then Micah met Jackson right after Easter eight months ago, and not only did his retired Dom side raise its head in interest, but the memories of Katarina resurfaced, along with all the old feelings of both.

Micah hadn't been looking for a mate when he found Jackson, not that that's how mating worked between members of their race. Vampires didn't just pick and choose who they wanted to mate with. Mother Nature did that for them. She decided when a mating link fired up and when it didn't, and one fired inside Micah for Jackson that night, even though Jack didn't experience the same response.

Micah still didn't understand why this had happened. Half-mating rarely occurred. In fact, Micah had only heard of it happening in rare cases involving mixed-bloods, not full-bloods, but he and Jackson were both one hundred percent vampire. Again, it just proved how different Micah was from everyone else. That he was an aberration. A weirdo anomaly.

A monster.

At first, Jackson had been ecstatic that Micah had bonded to him. He had heard about Micah in the circles he ran in… how Micah was revered by vampires and feared by drecks, and how he used to be a leather Lord who took his subs to unbelievable heights. For Jack, being seen with Micah was a major notch in his belt and a huge turn-on, but as the year now wound to a close, it was clear that Jack had merely used Micah for bragging rights.

Micah closed his eyes, sorrow ranging through him. Was he forever destined to be refuse? Nothing more than a token of misery? Had Katarina been the best part of him, and now he was nothing—less than nothing—without her? He could see the end coming with Jackson. He saw the thoughts that echoed from Jackson's mind. Now that the thrill was gone, and his itch had been scratched, Jackson was ready to move on to the next great conquest. He was a manipulator. Nothing more than a user. Lying through his mouth while his thoughts revealed the truth. Always in search of greener grass instead of cultivating what stood right in front of him.

Not even the realization that Jackson was a major asshole not worthy to be shit on would stop the *suffering* from taking hold when the time came for Jackson to leave. He had awakened Micah's urge to mate, and in doing so had opened up a door to Micah's past with Katarina. It was clear that when Jackson left—and he *would* leave, of that much Micah was certain—not only would Micah fall into *suffering* from the loss, but he would re-live the *suffering* he had experienced after Kat died.

Great. A fucking one-two punch. How would he survive this time? Would he even want to?

A chill ran down Micah's spine, more from the fear of what was to come than the cold, and he blinked his eyes open and surveyed the cityscape.

"Life goes on," he whispered sadly. "But not for me." This wasn't self-pity, but a weary ache of longing for the pain and suffering to end. For so long, he felt that all he had done was claw his way from one inner battle to the next only to get up night after night simply to exist. Yes, he was alive, but was he really living? Was he really keeping his promise to Katarina?

He sighed, so damn tired...ready to leave this life and enter the next. All around him, humanity stirred to a new day as the first hint of light crept up against the eastern horizon. Humans rose to get ready for work while vampires settled within the safety of their darkened confines to sleep away the sunlight. And drecks. Micah could smell their stench. They rotted the life from whatever and whomever they touched.

Right now, though, drecks were the least of his worries. Let them spread their repugnant stench in every alley and crevice of Chicago. He was checked out.

As if beckoned by Micah's taunts, movement caught his eye, and he rose to his feet as a Chicago police cruiser pulled to the curb in the distance. With his keen vision and sense of smell, Micah watched as a dreck disguised as a Chicago police officer stepped out of his patrol car.

John Apostle. That bastard.

The most nefarious drecks, Apostle included, posed as human law enforcement. The position gave them power they didn't inherently have and allowed them into places they otherwise wouldn't be able to go. Not to mention, posing as police officers put weapons in their hands, tapped them into the heartbeat and up-to-the-minute information of the city, which included activities vampires would rather keep secret, and put them within reach of criminals they could use for their connections, as well as for their own personal gain.

John Apostle had been on AKM's radar for years, but he proved a worthy adversary. They knew Apostle was up to no good and had ties to Royce, but they could never pin anything on him. The guy was cunning and covered his tracks better than Sasquatch.

Micah returned to his haunches as if Apostle would think to look to the top of The Sentinel and see him. What was Apostle doing in this part of town at this hour? This wasn't his normal beat. Micah would know. He had memorized the schedule of every dreck who worked on the police force, and he kept good tabs on them. Well, most of the time he did. Lately, with his Jackson troubles, he was slipping on his duties.

Two more drecks stepped from the shadows as Apostle approached. Even from here, he could tell they were drecks, even though they looked human.

Instinct and training took over, and Micah was about to mist himself closer to see if he could finally get something on that asshole when his skin prickled. He turned and found that the sun was beginning to crest the horizon.

Shit! Had almost an hour passed already?

Turning back toward Apostle, he frowned. He didn't have time to investigate and kick Apostle's ass into next season, which was unfortunate. He could use the exertion, but the sun demanded his return to his apartment. With one final glance at the drecks on the street, he projected himself inside.

Alone.

APOSTLE GLANCED LEFT AND RIGHT ALONG THE SIDEWALK. It was early morning. Too early for humans to be out in filthy droves, but late enough for the workaholics to already be in their offices or on their way there. This meant that the streets weren't completely void of life, but at least the vampires were down for the day.

Normally, he wouldn't venture this far north in the city, but he had a debt to collect. He brought his gaze back around to two of his dealers, Ovid and Regis.

"Apostle?" Ovid said cautiously.

"Ovid. Regis." He nodded to each in turn. "Let's go inside." Going indoors would get him out of the irritating, ass-frigid cold, but would also keep the rest of what was about to go down out of the public eye.

Ovid and Regis exchanged glances but turned and led him back inside the club they owned, which provided a nice front for cobalt distribution.

"What's up? What brings you around?" Regis said, but he spoke with the caution of someone who already knew why Apostle was there.

Apostle stepped around the bar and poured himself a beer, making himself at home. After all, Ovid and Regis only owned this bar by Apostle's good graces. He could do whatever the fuck he wanted, and if they had a problem with that...well, they *wouldn't* have a problem with that. Enough said. "How's business?" he said without answering Regis's question.

Restlessness worried Regis's body language, but Ovid tried to force a disarming smile.

Waste of time. Smiles didn't do much for Apostle. Cobalt sales, income to stuff in Premier Royce's coffers, and the weakening of the vampire race. That was what yanked Apostle's chain and gave him a mental hard-on. But a pansy-assed smile. Was Ovid serious?

"Business is good," Ovid said. "Better than ever."

Apostle took a drink of his beer as he came back around the counter and leaned against the bar. "Are you sure?"

"Oh yeah, yeah," Ovid said, flustered.

He calmly set down his mug. "Well now, that's interesting."

Ovid frowned, and Regis gulped uncomfortably. "Oh? Why?"

Apostle sighed. "You really think I'm stupid, don't you?"

Every once in a while, one of his teams of dealers got greedy, skimmed off the top, dipped their fingers too deeply into the profits that were supposed to go to Royce, and Apostle had to pay them a little visit and remind them who was in charge. Sure, a little skimming was natural. Cobalt dealers were greedy beings by nature, so he expected some five

DONYA LYNNE

fingering. He even padded the percentages to compensate for it. As it was, Ovid and Regis had been diving in a little *too* deeply. For months, the amount of cobalt they pushed into the hands of vampires didn't mesh with the dollars and cents being turned in, and every week saw a little bit more of a discrepancy, to the tune that O and R were in the hole about one hundred thousand dollars. It was time for a come-to-Jesus meeting.

"No, Apostle. Absolutely not," Ovid said.

Apostle pulled out his nightstick and slammed it into Ovid's gut before snaring his throat in his fist and shoving him against the wall. "You two owe me one hundred big ones. Did you really think I wouldn't notice? Did you really think I would just let that go?" He shifted to blue, and his eyes flashed red with a burst of anger. His long, blue-black hair hung well past his shoulders, and his fingers grew about an inch longer, his face hollowing out and growing gaunt.

Ovid struggled to speak against the hold Apostle had on his neck.

Regis sputtered from behind him, trying to find his voice, before spitting out, "We were going to pay it back. I swear."

God, Regis sounded like a sniveling human. No heart. No guts. Apostle released Ovid and spun, leveling Regis with a backhand that sent him sailing into a cocktail table ten feet away. "You most definitely *are* going to pay it back!" Anger flowed like lava through his veins. "Do you think I enjoy babysitting you fools? I could replace the two of you in an hour if I wanted to. Do you realize that?"

Regis gathered his bearings and stood, head down. He wouldn't even meet Apostle's eyes. Behind him, Ovid hacked and sputtered for air, and Apostle spun to face him. "You have one week to come up with the money. One week!"

Jesus! He felt like he was dealing with humans again. Before cobalt, the drecks' cash cows had been cocaine and heroin. Talk about fucking boring work. And a waste of energy. Cocaine and heroin were human recreational drugs. The shit did nothing to vampires. But since his brothers, Bishop and Deacon, had formulated cobalt, made from

57

dreck blood and dreck venom, they had a new weapon against their enemy. Not that it was much of a weapon, but anything that weakened the vampire race was a good thing. And cobalt did that, if only on a small scale. Vampires had begun to overdose on the stuff, and overdosing was good, because overdoses killed. If the drecks couldn't kill the vamps outright without violating the truce, then at least they could wipe them out chemically and claim it was their own fault, which kept the drecks' hands relatively clean.

But while the drugs continued to flow, the money had to do likewise. Bishop's operation didn't fund itself. So every now and again, Apostle had to play the heavy and send a message to his dealers not to get too greedy.

He only hoped Ovid and Regis took the hint. If they didn't, and he showed up next week and they didn't have the cash…? Well, put it this way, the race would be less two drecks. He *would* get his hundred Gs, even if it meant taking their lives and selling their assets for it.

CHAPTER 5

DECEMBER 15

A week after learning Josie was pregnant, Tristan still felt like he was in a dream, even though the doctor had confirmed yesterday that, yes, she was with child. What more evidence could he want? Josie was going to have his baby. They were going to be parents.

He was still grinning when his phone beeped a moment later.

"Yes?" he said.

"Your interview is here," the AKM receptionist said. "Severin Bannon."

Severin's file sat on Tristan's desk. The male looked impressive on paper. He was a former member of Vampire Dreck Affairs out of Atlanta and had an impressive résumé of human combat experience that would have filled a human soldier's uniform with enough ribbons to make a small table.

"Go ahead and bring him back." He had already mini-interviewed Severin on the phone, so the face-to-face was simply a formality, but a necessary one before adding him to the team.

A minute later, a knock came on his door, and he glanced up as the receptionist waved the broad-shouldered, long-haired male into his office.

"Severin? Pleasure to finally meet you." Tristan stood and extended his hand over his desk.

Sev locked him into a firm handshake. "Likewise, sir."

"Please, call me Tristan. We keep things pretty informal around here."

"Of course, and you can call me Sev."

Sev was a big fucker with friendly, if not a tad guarded, blue eyes that quickly scanned the room as if he was used to analyzing his surroundings. Probably a habit from his days as a member of the special forces in the human military. Wide in the shoulders with thick, heavily muscled arms and a long torso, Sev looked like he could lift a dump truck without breaking a sweat. Obviously, he could deliver the physical goods his résumé promised. And, damn! Tristan knew males and females alike who would kill for that head of long, blond hair that looked like something out of a Clairol commercial. Severin was sure to turn more than a few heads in Chicago.

"How was the drive up from Atlanta?" Tristan said as he gestured toward one of the chairs.

Sev took a seat. "Long."

"Did you drive straight through?" Sev's paperwork indicated he was a mixed-blood, which meant he was a day walker and could function in the daylight without cooking himself like barbecue. So, driving straight here during the day wouldn't have been a problem for him.

Sev nodded. "Yes. I was eager to get started."

Leaning back in his chair, Tristan laced his fingers in front of him. "Well, we're eager to get you started once you're settled. Do you have a place, yet?"

"I'm closing on a house tomorrow."

Tristan nodded. "Sounds like you're well ahead of the game."

"Yes, sir—sorry. Tristan."

He was going to like Severin. The guy was tough, experienced, and respectful, if not a bit on the quiet side. During their phone call, Sev didn't elaborate much on his personal life and gave short, concise answers. Not that Tristan got the impression Sev was being evasive. He just seemed like the type who kept his business private. Tristan respected that.

Tristan glanced at the guy's file. "It says here you were involved in the raid of that cobalt facility in Atlanta." He looked up as Sev shifted and grinned tightly. "I heard about that." A lot of Atlanta AKM enforcers had been killed in that raid. From the accounts Tristan had heard, the scene had been a bloodbath.

Sev cleared his throat. "Yes. I was working undercover there."

"What happened?"

With a shrug, Sev averted his gaze, clearly uncomfortable.

"I'm sorry," Tristan said. "If you don't want to talk about it—" It had to be hard to think about all the lives lost that day, some of whom Sev had probably known pretty well.

"No." Sev met his gaze. "I'm okay." He blinked several times and rubbed his palm over his face. "Shit just went way bad on that one is all. I wish I could have done more to stop it from happening, but..." He trailed off.

Tristan gave him a moment with his thoughts then asked, "Any idea who's funding these assholes?"

Sev shook his head, but there was something about his demeanor that made him appear uncomfortable, as if the memories of that day pained him. "No, but whoever it is, they've got a lot of disposable income. The drecks at that warehouse were well armed with some pretty impressive firepower you can't just buy at the local gun store. This was military grade."

"Yeah, that's what I heard." Tristan could tell the subject made Sev uneasy, which would explain why Sev had waited eight months to seek new employment. He had probably needed the time off to sort through the mental fallout. Somberness sank into the air, and Tristan's voice softened. "For what it's worth, I'm sorry you had to go through that. Clearly, you knew some of those who were killed."

Sev glanced at the floor and nodded sullenly. "One or two," he said quietly. "But life goes on, right?" He looked up again and forced a tight smile.

Tristan sat forward to rest his elbows on his desk. "If you're in this business long enough, you're bound to lose friends.

I've lost a few myself." One of which was still alive and on his team. Micah. Well, and Malek, but Malek had handled the death of his mate better than Micah had. But now wasn't the time to dwell on the emotional casualties on his own team. Hopefully, adding Sev would spark new life into the group. "I've been following the aftermath," he said of the Atlanta tragedy. "Premier Royce has been on King Bain's ass to find out who's killing the drecks who survived the raid. I don't know if you've kept up on the news, but someone has been hunting those drecks down one by one, and what's left behind isn't pretty." Since the raid, the surviving drecks were being systematically eliminated, as if by an assassin, which could be seen as a violation of the peace treaty if the assassin turned out to be a vampire, especially if said vampire worked for AKM.

Sev blinked again, and his jaw clenched. "Yes, I heard about that."

"Any ideas about who could be responsible?" Maybe Sev had seen something that could help them find this mysterious assassin. After all, he had been involved and had more firsthand knowledge of the raid than anyone else he had spoken to about it. "Did you see anyone suspicious? Did anything stand out as unusual?"

After a brief hesitation where he appeared to think about it, Sev shook his head. "No. Nothing."

Damn it. Tristan had hoped Sev could shed some light on the incident, as well as who had turned vigilante to hunt down the drecks who had survived. Looked like they were still at a loss, and Royce would just have to keep fuming. Oh well, there was nothing they could do about it tonight.

"Okay then," Tristan said, closing Sev's file with an air of finality. "How about we get you started right after the holiday? That'll give you a couple of weeks to get settled and catch your bearings before we start running you through the paces."

Sev looked relieved to abandon the subject of the Atlanta raid and clapped his hands on his thighs. "Sounds perfect to me. I'm eager to get back to work."

"Great. I'll get the paperwork started." Tristan stood. Sev joined him as they began for the door.

"I'm looking forward to working here, Tristan. The Chicago branch is the most active AKM facility in the world, and I'm ready to finally get back in the field. I haven't worked since leaving VDA eight months ago, and the down time is aggravating the shit out of me."

Tristan chuckled. "I know the feeling. I—" He cut off as Arion and Io entered the office and nearly crashed into them, caught up in conversation with one another.

"Oh, shit!" Arion said, bumping into Sev. He grabbed Sev's arms and took a step back. "Sorry." He glanced at Tristan, and Io stepped aside. "I didn't know you had company."

"Ari, this is Sev. Sev, this is Ari and Io. They're on the team."

Instant calm emanated from Sev as he extended his right hand toward Ari. "Hey."

Ari shook Sev's hand. "Hey. Good to meet you. You joining us?"

Sev nodded and took Io's outstretched hand, but didn't take his eyes off Ari. "Yes. After Christmas."

"Great. It'll be nice to have some new blood around here," Ari said.

"Just watch out for Micah," Io added as he released Sev's hand.

"Micah?" Sev looked between Io and Tristan. "Who's Micah? And why do I need to watch out for him?"

Ari chuckled. "You'll see, but don't let it sweat you."

Tristan sighed. "Micah is...well...he's different. And a little difficult to manage. But that's my job." Tristan placed his open palm on his chest. "But he's really a good guy." Ari scoffed, and Tristan threw him a warning glance. "He is. No matter what these two clowns say. You just need to get to know him."

"Yeah, right," Io said. "As if Micah would allow a newbie to get to know him."

Tristan shook his head, unable to hold back his own grin. Not that he liked talking ill about Micah, but the guy did bring it on himself. "Guys, come on. Don't scare Sev before he's even part of the team."

"It takes a lot more than that to scare me," Sev said, smiling. It was the first genuine smile Tristan had seen on Sev's face since he had arrived.

"Good," Ari said, chucking Sev's shoulder. "Then, welcome to the team. I can't wait to work with you and see what you've got." Ari's gaze swept over Sev's stacked shoulders and broad chest as if he were sizing up Sev's skills by his physique alone. Then he issued a friendly nod. "See you later." Ari paused for a heartbeat, met Sev's gaze, smiled, and then headed into the office with Io.

Sev watched him walk away, and then followed Tristan into the hall. "Nice guys."

Tristan regarded him. "Ari and Io?"

"Yeah. Ari seems friendly enough."

"He is. His father is one of King Bain's liaisons, so I think Ari gets his diplomatic skills from him. Io's a bit of a player, but damn, the guy can hack. Best hacker AKM's got. And Ari's his best friend. You never find one without the other."

Sev glanced over his shoulder toward Tristan's office as if he'd left something behind, but then turned back around and kept walking. "I'm looking forward to getting to know them better."

"Plenty of time for that. As for the other members on the team, there's Malek, Trace, and, of course, Micah. All good guys. Even Micah. He's just dealing with some heavy shit in his personal life right now." Understatement. "But if you want to learn from the best, it's him. Micah has been around a long time. Trained King Bain before he succeeded to the throne."

"No shit?" Sev sounded genuinely impressed.

Tristan chuckled. "No shit. He's solid. Definitely a male you want in your corner." Unless shit went south with Jackson, and then no one would want to be near Micah. Unlike Humpty Dumpty, no amount of help from all the king's men would help put Micah back together again if Jackson took off.

He walked Sev out and returned to his office to find that the rest of his team had shown up for their meeting. Even Micah. Surprise, surprise.

"Glad to see you tonight, Micah." He took his seat behind his desk. Micah hadn't attended a team meeting for a week. "I was beginning to think we'd lost you."

Micah sighed and slouched in his chair, legs stretched out in front of him, his fingers laced over his stomach as if he wanted to be anywhere else but there. "Can the bullshit, Tris." Then Micah's brow crinkled as his gaze slid up to meet Tristan's. As the two exchanged glances, Micah's eyes narrowed and his scowl deepened as he shifted and straightened in his seat. He looked like a jungle cat getting ready to pounce. Shit. What had Micah just picked up from his mind?

"Josie's pregnant?" The words left Micah's lips with an air of disbelief and something else. Loathing, maybe.

Tristan hadn't told the team, yet. He had planned to do that tonight. "Well, shit, Micah. Thanks for ruining my announcement."

Micah simply looked away, frowning. No apology. No congratulations. No nothing. Just apathy. Tristan understood Micah's reasons for his lack of interest. It had to be hell to desire something that badly and not get it, only to be reminded repeatedly—as others mated and had children—that he would always be left wanting. To hear that Josie was pregnant had to feel like a knife to Micah's gut.

The added torment was that Micah obviously wouldn't have any children of his own with Jackson, even if they stayed together, which was looking more and more like they wouldn't. So, yeah, Tristan's good news had likely ripped open old wounds that had never fully healed, and on top of everything going on with Jackson, hearing that Josie was pregnant probably sat as well on Micah's stomach as spoiled meat.

Off to the side, Trace watched Micah closely, as if he was aware of and concerned about Micah's inner turmoil. The rest of the team ignored Micah and offered their congratulations over the good news.

"How did that happen?" Malek asked, smiling.

Tristan shrugged. "I don't know. I guess I just got lucky."

Micah rolled his head around to glare at him. "Yeah. Lucky you."

Micah's anger and resentment were understandable. But just because Tristan understood Micah's pain didn't mean he had to quell his own excitement. And damn if he would let Micah steal his thunder on this, especially under the circumstances. For decades, Tristan had thought Josie would never have his baby, so he had every goddamn right to be happy and excited about the little miracle happening in his life right now. Screw Micah.

"Yeah, Tris," Ari said. "You're a lucky bastard. Not many males can say they're a dad when they haven't actually mated." He paused. "I hope I'm not that lucky. I don't need any rugrats running around."

Micah spit out a harsh laugh, shot Ari a glare, and then looked away.

"What?" Ari frowned at Micah.

"You're such an ass," Micah said. "You need to mate a *female* to produce *rugrats*, dumbass."

"What the fuck?" Ari said. "Where the hell did that come from? I'm perfectly aware of where children come from, asshole."

Io growled and sat forward. "Shut the fuck up, Micah. You're the dumbass around here."

Micah flipped Io off. "Don't worry, Io. I won't try to kiss your *boyfriend*." He glanced at Ari out of the corner of his eye as Ari's mouth fell open.

Io jumped out of his chair and jabbed a finger at Micah. "Fuck you, motherfucker! I don't go that way and you know it!"

"Mmm, you're turning me on, Io." Micah grabbed his crotch and blew Io a kiss then looked back at Ari. "That make you jealous, Ari? Me talking to your *boyfriend* like that? Blowing him kisses?" He chuckled…actually chuckled like he was in on some private joke.

Rage exploded as both Io and Ari went after Micah. Trace leaped from the wall and shoved Io back as Malek pulled Micah away.

Tristan had had enough. He jumped out of his chair, and

before anyone knew what was going on, he had Micah by the throat and dragged him away from the others. "I've had enough of your shit, Micah. You'd better calm the hell down and NOW!"

Micah snarled. "Or what? You'll pull rank on my ass and rip out my trachea? Go ahead. Do it." Blind fury with an edge of anguish shone from his navy blue eyes, and for an instant, Tristan felt as though Micah wanted him to do exactly what he'd just said, which would kill him. The look on Micah's face told Tristan all he needed to know about the state of Micah's relationship with Jackson. It was getting worse.

Part of Tristan—the new father he was going to be within the year—wanted to pull Micah in, hug him, tell him that everything was going to be okay. But hugs and consolation weren't Micah's thing. He was too macho for shit like that. Besides, hugs and sympathy weren't what Micah needed. That shit would only piss him off more. Still, Tristan didn't want to lose him. Micah had trained him, for God's sake. He was the toughest fucker Tristan had ever known, and he was the most lethal with a blade and a bow and arrow. The guy could hit a flea from fifty yards.

By rights, Micah should be in charge of the team right now, not Tristan. Hell, as brilliant as Micah was in the field and in matters of battle, he should be in charge of AKM, not just the team, but his mental state after Katarina's death had prevented his promotion. Time and again, as opportunities to advance within the King's Guard, which eventually became All the King's Men, presented themselves, Micah had been passed over. As those around him moved up in the ranks and took positions he should have filled, Micah remained a grunt, lagging behind because mated *suffering* compromised his mind, as well as his body. During the transition to AKM, Micah had only barely squeaked in as an enforcer, mostly on his reputation and his former relationship with King Bain, who refused to see Micah's skills wasted. Tristan felt nothing but respect for Micah, but respect only went so far when an inferno of misery smoldered from losing a mate, waiting for Jackson to leave so it could rekindle and burn Micah from the inside out this time.

"Micah, just cool off." Tristan pushed Micah away and turned his gaze on the others in the room. "Everybody else, shut up and sit down." The look he gave them must have conveyed his worry about Micah's mental state, because some of their bluster evaporated, and they slowly fell back into their respective spaces as Micah growled and backed toward the wall near Trace, who kept a watchful eye on him.

A few tense moments ticked by, but when no one mouthed off or took a swing at anyone else, Tristan finally sat back down. "Okay, now that we're all better"—he arched an eyebrow at Micah, and then at Ari and Io—"we can get started. As you already found out from blabbermouth, Josie's pregnant. We found out a week ago."

Subdued congratulations rose again from everyone except Micah. Well, and Trace, who simply nodded and slipped a matchstick between his lips like it was a toothpick.

"She's due next August, and, depending on how things go, I might need to take time off occasionally to tend to her." It was the male's duty to take care of his female during pregnancy, so Tristan would be given a long leash for the next nine months. "When that happens, *Malek* will be in charge." He shot Micah a glance as if he expected him to protest, but his dark-haired mentor kept his gaze on the floor, frown firmly in place, arms crossed defiantly over his broad chest. The guy was like a rock, both solid and apathetic, as if being passed over yet again in the rank and file didn't bother him, but Tristan knew it had to grate Micah's nerves to be notched ever lower in the pecking order. Setting Micah on the sidelines as merely an enforcer and not a leader was like benching the star quarterback, but what else could Tristan do? Micah was in no shape to run himself, let alone a team. "What do you think of Malek being in charge, Micah?" he said warily, feeling the need to get Micah's acceptance directly rather than leave it to chance. It was Tristan's decision to make, but when it came to Micah, sometimes it was better to include the guy in the decisions...or at least make it *seem* like he was being included.

Micah shrugged one shoulder and met his gaze with empty eyes then glanced at Malek with a nod. "Malek's capable." His voice had dropped and grown hoarse as if he'd just shot up on heroin. "He's a solid choice."

Malek and Micah had been best friends once, which was another reason why Tristan wanted Malek in charge if he had to take time off to be with Josie. There was a greater chance Micah wouldn't be a total asshole to Malek, who he showed a certain amount of respect. If anyone else was left in charge, that probably wouldn't be the case.

"Malek? You good with that?" Tristan turned his gaze to his new second-in-command.

Malek nodded acceptance. "You can count on me."

Yes, Tristan could count on Malek. Despite the fact that he had lost his mate, Carmen, around the same time Micah had lost Katarina, he still had his wits about him. For whatever reason, Malek had dealt better with his loss. The guy was still a bundle of dysfunction on a lot of levels, and he seemed to be as apathetic as Micah when it came to relationships, because he hadn't been with a woman since Carmen died, but at least he kept his head about him when it came to work.

"Good. That's settled." Tristan scrawled his signature on the form that secured Malek as his replacement and set it aside to hand over to administration later. "Okay. Next order of business. Two drecks turned up dead this morning. Human law enforcement found them, but once they hit our database, flags went up. We sent a team of day walkers over to grab them and wipe out the records." Tristan opened another file. "Names were Orvis and Regis. Cobalt dealers. They ran Azure, that night club on the North Side."

"I saw John Apostle there a week ago," Micah said.

Everybody appeared shocked that Micah had spoken, and honestly, Tristan was, too. Lately, Micah had been more the type to sit and brood silently than offer input. Tristan leaned back in his chair and faced Micah. "John Apostle?" They could never get proof that Apostle was up to no good, even though everyone knew he was. That bastard covered his tracks better than a fairy in the woods. If Apostle had been at Azure, it was a good bet he hadn't been there to drink and dance, especially with Orvis and Regis showing up dead a week later.

"Do you know what he was doing there?"

Micah shook his head, arms still crossed, expression indifferent. "No."

"Did you hear what he talked to them about?"

Micah sighed and pinched the bridge of his nose as if he were only just barely holding his tongue from another smart-assed outburst. "I wasn't close enough." He looked like he was only marginally holding himself together, so Tristan decided not to push for more. Micah waved toward the file on Tristan's desk. "But I can guess now that Beavis and Butt-Head showed up dead."

Malek sat forward in his chair. "Apostle has a reputation for being especially hard to work for. Brutal, unforgiving, a real prick. And we've seen this before. He pays his dealers a visit, and a few days to a few weeks later, the dealers he visited wind up dead. Maybe Orvis and Regis had fucked up on a sale, or maybe they owed Apostle money, and this was his way of sending a message to the others."

"Could be," Tristan said, "but we don't even know for sure if it was Apostle who killed them. With all due respect to Micah," he said as he nodded toward Micah, "Apostle being there last week could just be a coincidence." He paused, preparing for the pending outburst. "Since they were drecks, we need to investigate. And it's our team's turn in the rotation."

Groans rose from everyone except Micah and Trace. This was the one part of the job no one liked, but since AKM was responsible for maintaining the truce between the two races, it was their job to investigate any dreck deaths of a questionable nature, and the teams rotated the duty on a weekly schedule.

"I'll take it," Micah and Malek both said at the same time. They looked at each other. Micah's brow crinkled over his nose as he frowned, and Malek's jaw clenched.

"Good," Tristan said before either could back out. "Both

of you. Take it. I'll email you the files after the meeting." He handed the file to Malek. "Work it up. See what you can find."

Tristan knew it was a shit detail without a lot of hope of turning up much, but if there was anything to find, Micah and Malek would find it. They worked well together, despite Micah's chronically foul temperament and his reluctance to work with anyone. He preferred solo patrol, and Tristan usually allowed it, but not this time.

"Last order of business," Tristan said before dismissing everyone. "King Bain's Christmas party."

Everyone quieted, and Ari grinned. His father had probably already told him that their team had been drawn in this year's lottery.

Tristan smiled. It was nice to give them good news once in a while. "Our team is invited this year."

Not every team was able to attend the king's holiday party, which was a grand affair that included dignitaries, his liaisons, VIPs, and a cavalcade of who's who in their world. Since AKM had to continue operating, Bain held a lottery to determine which teams were able to attend. For those who couldn't, he sent in a catered meal and enough generic gifts that everyone received one.

Ari and Io high-fived, and Tristan could almost see Io's mind reeling over all the fresh female meat he could seduce.

Tristan would nip that in the bud right now. "Io, you're to conduct yourself in a manner fit for royalty, do you hear me? I don't want the king or anyone else coming back to me this year complaining about your behavior with any of the females in attendance the way they did the last time we attended one of the king's holiday parties." Tristan raised an expectant brow at him.

Io mock saluted, but the self-ingratiating grin splattered on his face said he was looking forward to having a more exclusive bounty of females to choose from. God, but Io was a womanizing SOB. And Ari wasn't much better, easily the best looking guy on the team. Females both vampire and human flocked to them everywhere they went, but at least Ari was more of a gentleman. He remained cordial, never appearing as into them as Io was. But to say Io was into women was like saying bees were into honey. Io was indiscriminate, stealing hearts everywhere he went and leaving them crushed an hour later. It didn't matter where he was when he found a woman he wanted. He dragged her into the nearest restroom or back alley and, with unceremonious disrespect, fucked her against the wall or the stall's door, and left her there with a smile on her face as he returned to whatever he was doing before. Sometimes he even wiped his memory from them so they wouldn't get *leachy*, as he called it. Io wasn't into hangers-on. Love 'em and leave 'em fast was his motto. Get in, get out, and get on to the next. If there was one male on his team that Tristan thought would never take a mate, it was Io. He just wasn't the type, and Tristan couldn't see it happening. He was too interested in the next conquest…and the next after that.

Note to self. Remind Io who the king's daughter is so he doesn't mistake her for a guest and paw her in the coat closet.

"I mean it, Io. Don't embarrass me or the team."

Io grinned at Ari again, but nodded. "I'll be good." He leaned toward Ari and whispered loud enough for everyone to hear, "*Real* good. Right, buddy?"

Ari sighed and rolled his eyes, but didn't meet Io's gaze. "As always."

Great. Tristan would have to keep an eye on Io at the party. He couldn't afford losing the guy if he happened to seduce the wrong female, and there would be plenty of wrong females there to seduce.

"Well, anyway, the date for the party is Christmas Eve. Dress code—do I really need to remind everyone to wear a suit and tie? Maybe even a tuxedo if you want to really impress the king." He glanced around the room, his gaze landing on Trace. Did that guy even own a tie? "But in years past, people have shown up in nice sweaters and slacks, too. Just make sure you don't show up looking like a gangbanger or a thug." Trace was the only one Tristan was worried about. Tristan had never seen Trace wear anything but cargo pants, jeans, and T-shirts that showed off his impressive chest and arms. And maybe an occasional beat-up sweatshirt with a tattered collar and a bleach stain or two. Trace didn't exactly scream fashion diva...or even fashion literate. He seemed more into practical comfort and functionality. Even so, Trace didn't flinch when Tristan announced the dress code for the party. Hmph. Maybe Trace would shock the shit out of him and show up in a tux with tails and a top hat. Wouldn't that be something?

"Any questions?" Tristan said.

Silence answered him.

"Good. Let's go. Malek? Micah? Get on that and let me know what you find." He nodded toward the file in Malek's hand. "Io, see what you can dig up on Azure. If they had security cameras, I want to see whatever you can get me from the last week. Hack into CPD and see what they got at the scene." He considered what Malek had mentioned earlier. "And get me Azure's financial records. And look into Orvis's and Regis's personal records, too. See if you can find anything that looks suspect." Doubtful. Drecks were good at covering up their illicit activity, but once in a while, AKM struck gold, which made the effort worthwhile. "Trace, you and Ari canvas the area around Azure. Ask around. See if you can pick up anything that could help." Again, it was doubtful they would turn up anything more than speculation, but they had to perform their due diligence. "That's it." He slapped his palms on his desk. "Oh. One more thing. We've got a new team member joining us after Christmas. Severin Bannon. He's a day walker who worked for Vampire Dreck Affairs in Atlanta and has an impressive background in the human military. SEAL. Green Beret. The guy's a real machine. I'll send his file to you all shortly."

Ari bobbed his head in agreement. "He's impressive. Big guy. Io and I met him before the meeting."

Micah smirked as if he knew a secret, but he kept his mouth shut.

"Be ready to put him through the paces," Tristan said. "He'll get a turn with all of you."

Micah actually smiled, his gaze still on Ari.

"Something funny, Micah?" Tristan said.

Micah's gaze slid to his. "Nope. Just looking forward to meeting him."

"You?" Ari frowned up at him.

"You got a problem with that, Ari?" Micah's eyes were full of mischief. "Me and Severin?"

Ari scowled back at him and shook his head. "Fuck off, dick spill. I'm not going to play your stupid mind games." Ari dismissed Micah with a wave of his hand and pushed himself out of his chair.

Micah chuckled wryly then turned for the door as if he knew the meeting was over. Clearly, whatever was going on between him and Ari would remain his secret, which was fine by Tristan.

Furniture rustled, and the members of his team filed out, leaving Tristan alone. He smiled at his phone, which rested on the upper left corner of his brown desk blotter, and picked it up. He sent Josie a text.

"I love you."

A few seconds later, his phone vibrated and he read her reply.

"I love you, too. You're going to make a great daddy."

Damn straight he would. Dysfunctional team meeting from hell aside, right now Tristan was the luckiest guy in the world.

CHAPTER 6

AT 1:00 A.M., Micah glanced at Malek in the passenger seat. They'd gotten nowhere with the investigation of the drecks' murders, and a sweep of the vics' homes had only revealed more of the same.

"What say we can this investigation and head to the Garter?" Micah said.

Already, Micah could feel his sanity slipping. He'd been an ass at AKM tonight. He knew he was already the least favorite member of the team as far as the rest were concerned. Why Tristan continued to put up with him was a mystery, but he usually kept his ill temper to himself.

He'd had no right ripping into Ari and Io the way he did. Thanks to Jackson and the impending end of their relationship, he was becoming even less cordial and more temperamental than usual. He wasn't fooling himself about that, and if he could, he would break it off first, but doing that was akin to peeling off his own fingernails one by one. Or cutting off his own leg. A mated male just didn't break up with the one he had mated. That kind of shit didn't happen. Vampire matings weren't like human marriages, which could be dissolved without so much as a blink. No. Vampires mated on a level so deep that for a male to lose a mate often meant death. And since Micah had already lost one mate, losing another was probably going to kill him. Which meant this was probably the last opportunity he would have to spend with Malek before he lost his sanity…and most likely his life.

Malek glanced across the seat at him. "Micah, we've got work—"

Micah held up his hand and cut him off. "Dumb and Dumber aren't going to mind if we cut out an hour or two early." He tapped the file sitting on the console between them. "It's not like they'll spring back to life if we put in our full shift."

"Micah." A warning tone edged Malek's voice, but compassion dwelled there, too.

"Malek…" Micah met his gaze for a split second, and then turned his attention back to the road. He needed this time with his oldest and dearest. Not that he would spill his guts and beg absolution for all the sins he'd committed in the last thousand years, because, let's face it, he wasn't into spilling. The two of them could just sit in silence the whole time for all Micah cared. That was fine by him. He needed this. And when he was gone, Malek would understand that Micah had wanted to leave him with something good. One last memory to remind him that, at one time, Micah had been a good guy. A male of integrity and compassion who sought the best in people. Who lent a hand to those in need. Selfless and giving. Not the male he had become after Katarina's death. Not the male who left a lot to be desired now.

Malek would understand when Micah was gone that his suggestion tonight was a gift meant expressly for him… something for Malek to hold on to and take strength from in the days to come.

Something in his tone—or maybe even his expression—got through, and Malek nodded. "Okay. Let's go. It won't hurt if I'm a few days early, anyway."

Malek went to the Black Garter one night a month. Only one. That was all the sexual exposure he allowed himself, and even so, his visits were only to watch. He never picked up a woman. He hadn't taken a female home in centuries. Not since Carmen's death. How he managed to keep a cap on his *suffering* and not lose his mind was something Micah had never figured out. Malek had tucked away Carmen's memory and worshipped it as if they were still together, even though on the conscious level, he knew she was gone.

Weren't the two of them a pair? He and Malek were the

two most broken and maladjusted members of Tristan's team, except that Malek had handled the loss of his mate better than Micah had. It was the only thing that distinguished them from one another.

More than one person had asked if he and Malek were brothers, they looked so much alike. Both had long, dark, almost black hair, and they both had striking facial features, although Malek had softer edges. Micah's face was all hard, severe angles. And where Micah had navy blue eyes that were so dark they almost looked black, Malek had brown eyes. Back before they'd met Katarina and Carmen, they'd been quite the popular pair, catching maidens' eyes everywhere they went, often landing in their beds.

Now look at them. Micah was a sexual deviant, and Malek was celibate. Oh, what the passage of time can do to a person.

He turned the SUV around and headed in the direction of the Garter as light snow began to fall. Fifteen minutes later, he pulled into the parking lot, and he and Malek headed through the front door into the elegant vestibule, with its scantily clad hostess and her well-dressed bodyguard. Well, he was probably more like a bouncer, but with his crisp, black suit and red, silk tie, he looked more like a member of the Secret Service than the bouncer of a gentlemen's club. And underneath that suit coat, he was probably packing firepower worthy to protect the president. The Garter's owner protected his girls. This wasn't the place for rowdy or boisterous bill waving and cat calls. The patrons treated the dancers with respect, or they got the boot and weren't allowed back.

Micah and Malek paid their entry fee and made their way through the long, dimly lit hall toward the main room, where sultry, bass-heavy music provided the soundtrack for the dancer on stage. A long, meticulously appointed bar stretched along the left wall, and cocktail waitresses dressed in various negligees came and went with drinks for the patrons.

The place was packed tonight, so Micah turned his mental abilities on a man who sat at a table midway to the stage. With a thought, he influenced the man to vacate his seat, and he and Malek quickly slid in to take his place. Humans were so easy to manipulate.

The Black Garter's setup was made more for the single observer or small groups than larger ones, and the recessed floor surrounding the main stage held only small tables with no more than two upholstered easy chairs apiece. In the back and along the walls were tables and booths for groups of four or more, but if you wanted close to the action, you came alone or with no more than one other person.

Then, of course, were the VIP rooms for bachelor parties.

However, what many men liked about the Garter were the rooms in back where they could buy a private dance with one of the girls. Micah had used those rooms a time or two, where the rules were a little more lax than out here in the public, but the girls were still treated respectfully.

Micah was in the mood for a private dance tonight. It might help take his mind off Jackson.

"What can I get you boys?"

He looked up into the heavily made up eyes of a blonde with surgically enhanced breasts as she stood between him and Malek, tray in hand. She wore a black, silk teddy.

"Lagavulin on the rocks, please," Malek said with only a cursory perusal of her outfit.

"Same for me." Micah appraised her legs. She did have nice legs. "And can you tell me if Scarlet is dancing tonight?"

She smiled politely and winked. "She sure is, honey. She'll be dancing soon."

Micah stopped her before she could walk away to get their drinks. "I'd like to buy a private dance with her."

Her smile turned upside down in a pouty display of sympathetic refusal. "Scarlet's already booked up tonight, honey, but Sasha's got a couple more openings for privates. How does that sound?"

Micah shook his head, disappointed. "No, thank you. Maybe I'll catch Scarlet next time." Scarlet was the only dancer he wanted to buy a private dance from, and it wasn't because she was the Garter's primary dancer. He was drawn to her...had been ever since the first time he'd seen her dance the night he met Jackson. And despite the bond that had formed with Jackson, Micah had still come back here to see Scarlet dance occasionally. But the couple of times he had tried to buy a private with her, she'd been booked. Looked like he would have to end his days without her special attention.

"I'll take one of those openings with Sasha," Malek said to the waitress, and he turned over his credit card.

Malek wasn't as particular as Micah, but then he only wanted the private performance so he could jack his rocks off when he got home. Not that Micah was criticizing, because he wasn't. This was just how Malek coped with his *suffering,* and since Malek never criticized Micah about how he handled his own shit, Micah wouldn't disparage Malek for how he handled his.

"Sure thing, honey." She winked and smiled again. "I'll be right back with your drinks."

The dancer on stage ended her performance, and four others took up the smaller spotlight platforms on either side of the main stage and in the back of the room.

"So," Malek said, "What's up with you and Jackson?"

Micah's pulse went from zero to sixty in half a second. If it had been anyone else asking—especially that closeted nosebug Arion—Micah would have told him to fuck off and mind his own business, but this was Malek, who only had Micah's best interests in mind. Micah clamped down his irritation.

"Nothing."

Malek regarded him with a cautious if not curious sidelong glance. "Nothing, huh?"

He never had been able to lie to Malek. With a sigh, he flexed his shoulders and shifted in his chair. "He's going to leave me."

At least Malek had the courtesy to look away. Mating shit wasn't such a pretty topic between them. "I'm sorry, man."

Their waitress returned with their drinks and set them on red cardboard coasters outlined with the image of a lacy black garter. "Your private with Sasha is at two fifteen," she told Malek.

He accepted his receipt. "Thank you."

After she left, Micah leaned forward, elbows on the table as if hugging his drink. He turned toward Malek. "When he leaves, I don't want you or anyone else to see me."

Malek's gaze met his, and a sober moment of understanding passed between them. "You gonna be all right?"

Micah glanced away. He already knew he wouldn't be. When Jackson left him, he would be fucked. As in way fucked. Up shit creek without a paddle. Crossing the River Styx without a token for Charon would be easier. He would be stuck in everlasting purgatory and hell all mixed into one. "Yeah. Sure." He lifted his glass to his lips and sipped. "But I'll be fucked up. You saw how I was with Kat."

"Yeah. I did."

When Micah looked back at Malek, his old friend's expression—along with the thoughts of doubt rolling through his mind—told him he wasn't buying Micah's load of shit. He slumped his shoulders and looked into his liquid amber. "I'm not stupid, Malek," he said softly. "I know I'm in trouble. Big trouble. Jackson..." He closed his eyes and took a heavy breath before continuing. "Mating Jackson has awakened everything I felt for Kat after she died. It's like I'm feeling it all over again." He slowly swirled his drink, making the ice clink the sides of the glass. "And he doesn't love me. He never did. I can hear his thoughts and know there's someone else. I see what they do with one another, but there's nothing I can do to stop him, and yet I can't walk away." He lifted his gaze to Malek's and saw complete and total understanding reflected back at him. Like any other male of their species, Malek knew Micah was between the proverbial rock and a hard place. Micah looked back down into his glass. "It's just a matter of time, Malek." A matter of time before his mental faculties short-circuited and tossed him like a rag doll into *suffering* so intense he'd be lucky to remember his own name when the end came.

Malek's hand squeezed his shoulder, and Micah looked up into eyes filled with compassion. "Is there anything I can do?" Malek said.

Micah offered him a sad grin and shook his head. "Just make sure no one sees me like that. Keep them away. You stay away, too. I don't want to hurt you or anyone else." He fixed Malek with a serious stare. "I mean it, Malek. Don't you come looking for me. We clear?"

Malek blinked once and let his gaze fall to the table. When he spoke, his voice was soft but resigned. "We're clear."

Breathing more easily, Micah pulled away and leaned back in his chair, drink in hand. "You're the only one I trust with this, Malek. The only one I can count on."

"I know. And I won't let you down."

Micah nodded tightly and kept his gaze averted. "Thank you."

Silence filtered into the space between them, and they pretended to watch the dancers on either side of the stage, but Micah's mind was elsewhere. It was as if an hourglass sat over his soul, counting down to destruction. When he met Jackson and formed the one-sided tether to him, Jackson had been like a clear blue sky after a late summer storm, letting the sunlight shine onto the newly brightened landscape. Now, their relationship *was* the storm.

Micah glanced out of the corner of his eye toward Malek, who, on the outside, feigned interest with the stripper to the left of the stage, but his mind was a tidal wave of emotion. Malek knew that, in his way, Micah had just said good-bye, and a thousand good memories of the time they had spent together before losing their mates so long ago trained through his thoughts.

Back in the time of King Bain the First, he and Malek had spent countless nights in pubs and inns where they watched females dance and sing for their entertainment, and where they partook of feminine desire and pleasure upstairs in one of the many private bedrooms. That had been where Micah had learned how to be with a woman. Where he had been taught how to touch a female, kiss her, and delight in what she offered. And he had taken his education home to Katarina at the end of that first war.

God, how he'd loved Katarina. But she was gone, and it

looked like he would be joining her soon.

The lights dimmed, and the music faded, bringing Micah's mind back to the Garter as the hard synthesized beats of White Zombie's "More Human than Human" pulsed out of the speakers. A few seconds later, the MC, hidden somewhere off stage said, "Gentlemen...Scarlet." It was all the introduction she needed.

The curtain opened, and Scarlet rested in a curled position, head down, her long black hair—most likely a wig—hung down like drapes to hide her face. She was the sexiest damn creature Micah had seen in forever. That woman could dance. And stretch. And flex. And work a stripper pole like no one's business. Micah went stiff at the thought of her riding up and down his body the way she did that damn pole, which was odd since most mated males didn't get turned on by anyone other than their mate. Then again, Scarlet was a woman worth getting hard over. She never failed to arouse him. As in really arouse him. Heck, maybe the fact that he had first seen her dance on the same night that he had met Jackson had somehow linked him to her. After all, she had been the reason he'd gone in search of relief that night in the first place. He had been lustfully roused by her performance to the point of distraction, and after trying to buy a private dance with her to explore the possibilities between them further, he had come away disappointed, because her schedule had been full. Same as it was tonight and the other times he had come here. He couldn't get here early enough to get on the woman's calendar, so he was relegated always to be part of a crowd instead of an audience of one.

As the first slide of electric guitar screamed from the speakers, Scarlet, dressed in a sexy white jumper, slid up from the floor to her feet as she eased the zipper down on the front of the jumpsuit, and then she flipped her head back, sending her long tresses flying to reveal her face. As usual, she wore a mask, which made her allure even more appealing. What looked like a contraption he might find in his long-abandoned dungeon covered her mouth. It looked like a muzzle, made of solid, black material that resembled plastic. And over her eyes was a thin strip of leather, like a Bat Boy mask. Eyeholes revealed her vivid, green eyes, which seemed to lock to his briefly as she peeled out of her jumpsuit like a sexy kitten.

Damn. Underneath, she wore only a modern, almost tech-looking, black-and-white bikini, accented with white plastic over black spandex that clung in all the right places and left little to the imagination.

Clear, hard plastic stripper shoes that looked like glass, with two-inch platform soles, led up to long, lean legs, and Micah briefly pictured those legs around his hips, her body under his on his bed, her fingers digging into his back as she cried his name. He blinked and shook his head. That image was way too real. Almost like a premonition. What the hell?

Scarlet worked the room like a maestro. Everyone came to the Garter to see her, which was why management usually pushed her show toward the end of the evening to keep the patrons hanging and spending. And tonight was no exception. The room was packed even more now than before. Standing room only.

Scarlet gripped the pole, swung around, upside down, and contorted herself into positions worthy of Cirque du Soleil. God, she was one fucking flexible human being, and Micah's cock twitched as another shot of her getting flexible on him in his bedroom dashed through his mind.

Who knew what to expect from Scarlet? Sometimes her shows were softer, more angelic. Sometimes they were more classical. Then others, like tonight, she was hard and in your face, almost like an angry, bondage queen ready to pull out a whip and draw blood. She leaped off the pole, sank into a power squat, rotated her hips hard, arms strong and flexed, head back as if she were pleasuring herself to orgasm, and then she whipped herself around the pole again, her body all hard angles and strength.

If men here cheered, they would be losing their voices right about now. Because, shit, Scarlet was hotter than Hades, on fire beyond the usual. Maybe it was the heavy-duty beats she cavorted to, because White Zombie provided a raw soundtrack for the extreme moves she was laying down, and Micah sat transfixed, taking in this last bit of enjoyment.

All too soon, the song ended, and Scarlet bowed and left the stage. And for what felt like the first time in almost five minutes, Micah breathed. She had that effect on him, and as he glanced around the room and picked up the vibe of heavy arousal from the crowd, it was clear he wasn't the only one she affected.

Possessive jealousy hummed under his skin, and he glared at the other patrons, ready to rip off the heads of anyone who tried to touch her.

What the fuck? Why was he going all mated male medieval all of a sudden? He was already mated—well, half-mated—to unreciprocating Jackson. His reaction to Scarlet didn't make sense.

Out of the corner of his eye, he saw Malek check his watch. It was almost time for his private dance. "You sticking around?" Malek said.

Micah shook off the odd mated aggression roiling through his nerves…emotions that Scarlet, not Jackson, had evoked. "No, man. I'm going to get out of here." He needed to clear his head, get some fresh air, move, do something. Because his brain was fritzing out.

"You sure?" Malek stood and downed the rest of his drink before setting the empty glass back on the table.

"Yeah, I'm sure." Micah adjusted himself, killed his own drink, and dropped a twenty on the table to cover their bill as he stood.

"Okay." Unspoken promises thickened the air between them. Promises of good-bye and secrecy, as well as protection. Malek would keep his word and not let anyone come for Micah when Jackson left. "You take care, Micah."

"You, too, Malek." He clasped hands with his old friend. Then he pulled away and headed for the door as Malek slinked toward the private rooms in back, a shroud of guilt falling over him. The guy still felt like he was cheating on Carmen, and Micah stopped for a moment and stared with compassion after him. Poor Malek. What would happen to him after Micah was gone?

Outside, the snow had picked up, coming down in blustery curtains of large, heavy flakes, coating the sidewalks and streets with over an inch of powder. Within minutes, Micah's hair was covered, as were his shoulders.

He didn't mind the cold, so he kept walking. A couple of times, he felt eyes on him, but when he stopped and searched the shadows, he saw no one. It was probably nothing. He'd been feeling watched for weeks now, but no one was ever there when he looked, and if someone really was tailing him, wouldn't he have revealed himself by now? So, yeah, the sense of being watched had to be all in his head, even though his instincts told him otherwise.

He didn't know how long he had been walking—a long time, though—when he lifted his gaze and found himself approaching Berlin, the club where he had met Jackson. That had been a strange night. He'd been in an especially foul mood, kicked off his shift early, stopped by the Garter, drooled over Scarlet, and then found himself here as he searched for someone to ease the ache in his balls when Scarlet had been unavailable. Berlin was known for its gay and lesbian patronage, so why he had ended up here that night was a question he couldn't answer. But he had, and Jackson had made eye contact with him from the dance floor, where he'd been grinding up on some other guy. It had been instant attraction between them. Jackson ended up ditching his dance partner, cozied up to Micah at the bar, and the two of them had ended up in the men's room, with Jackson on his knees in front of him and Micah's hands fisting Jackson's dark brown hair. Micah hadn't intended for it to be anything more than a casual one-nighter, but the rest that happened between them had been history from that moment on.

And now their relationship was history. They fought too much, and unlike others who argued, he and Jackson had stopped making up. There were no more apologies. No more requests for forgiveness. No makeup sex. No sex at all. Jackson's needs were getting satisfied elsewhere. The guy enjoyed fucking too much to have gone celibate altogether, and Micah had already seen in Jack's mind what he was doing and where and with whom he was spending his nights.

Speak of the devil. Micah's heart lurched as if stabbed as Jackson spilled from Berlin's doors in the arms of another male. A human. The one Micah had seen in Jackson's thoughts. The two hesitated then locked into a passionate kiss, arms squeezing each other, hands groping body parts that had been meant for Micah. Even from over a block away, the smell of Jackson's arousal stung Micah's nostrils.

His mated male side roared to life, just as it had with Scarlet a little while ago. That was his mate, goddamn it! How dare he find pleasure with another! How dare that human grope what belonged to him! And unlike with his reaction to Scarlet, he would do something about this betrayal, goddammit!

Micah was about to barrel in and strangle the asshole groping Jackson's crotch and sticking his tongue down his throat when a hand closed around his wrist.

"Hey, Mike. What's up?"

Micah spun to find Traceon, that quiet, dark-skinned mixed-blood who always stood off to the side chewing a matchstick during team meetings, standing beside him. His pale green eyes scrutinized him, narrow and shrewd. Trace hadn't missed anything. He knew what Micah was up to.

"What are you doing here?" Micah snapped, yanking his arm away. He looked back up to find that Jackson and his new beau were gone.

"Following a lead." Trace's deep voice held no emotion. No inflection. It was almost monotone. "Where's Malek?"

Micah began walking toward Berlin's front entrance, searching for Jackson. "Who are you, my mother?"

Trace fell into step beside him. "Not since the last time I checked."

Micah regarded him with a sidelong glance. "What are you doing?"

"What do you mean?"

"Are you following me?" He thought about his odd feelings

of being watched lately and wondered if Trace was to blame. The guy did come pre-packaged with special gifts, being that he was a mixed-blood. Maybe one of his gifts included being able to hide in the shadows. No one knew for sure. Trace never talked about himself and kept his life pretty hushed and closed off. And his mind was like a locked box. For all the chatter Micah picked up from everyone else, he never got shit from Trace.

Trace flicked his gaze at him with a crooked frown. "Following you? I was about to ask if you're following me."

Micah tried to get inside Trace's head, but as usual, the mental fortress surrounding Trace's thoughts was firmly in place. He'd never met someone who could so easily close him off like that. Most of the time, people's minds were an open book. He didn't even have to try—he simply heard their thoughts. It could be exhausting, but he had learned to adjust to the odd-even-for-a-vampire phenomenon a long time ago.

"Why would I want to follow you?" Micah scowled and picked up his pace. He didn't want Trace around. Couldn't the guy take a hint?

"Exactly my thought," Trace said, meeting him stride for stride.

Micah searched the encroaching crowd for Jackson, but he was gone. His scent lingered, but it seemed he and his human had already split. Sudden aggression surged through his blood. Jackson was with someone else, heading off to do God knew what to one another. His heart splintered as anger, humiliation, and hopelessness crashed together like fusion atoms.

Roaring, he spun on Trace, grabbed him by the throat, and slammed him into the nearest brick wall, lifting him off the ground. "What the fuck do you want, Trace?"

Trace closed his eyes, almost as if he enjoyed the pain, and then blinked them open again to meet Micah's gaze. "Walk away from him, Micah." He spoke as calmly as he could with Micah's fist around his neck.

Micah reared back, and the skin around his eyes pinched and tightened as he glared at him. "Who are you talking about?"

"You know who I'm talking about." Trace's expression grew deathly serious. "Walk away, Mike. He's only going to hurt you."

Micah slammed him against the wall again, and Trace sighed and dreamily closed his eyes before lazily lifting his lids. The corners of his mouth curled as if he'd just had a hit of feel-good juice. What the hell was up with this guy? Did he get off on pain or something? "Don't pretend to know what's going on here, Trace."

It looked like Trace had to force himself to focus. "I'm not pretending to know anything."

"Like fuck you aren't."

Trace waved his right hand, and Micah felt a wave of calming energy pour over him. It was enough to make him loosen his grasp and let Trace drop to the ground. Micah's gaze fell to Trace's hand then lifted again to meet his eyes. Trace had just gotten infinitely more interesting, but he was still wading in murky waters where Micah was concerned, and Trace needed to get out of his business before he lost a body part. What did Trace know about anything, anyway? He wasn't mated and never had been. "I'm going to ask you again, Trace. Are you following me?"

Trace exhaled heavily, and his breath formed a fog of vapor in the cold air. Then he pushed his skull cap more securely over his hairless melon and glanced up the snow-covered sidewalk as a sharp wind drove against them. "What you need is a guardian angel, Micah." Trace flashed him a quick glance, and then he turned and trudged away, head down, hands buried in his coat pockets, leaving large, heavy footprints in the snow.

"I don't need shit, Trace. Least of all a guardian angel. So fuck off and leave me alone." Micah checked the time. It was after four in the morning. He still had a few hours before sunrise, but he no longer felt like being out and about. He wanted to go home. Where he could drown himself in a drunken haze.

His time was running out.

CHAPTER 7

TRISTAN GRUNTED AND DROVE HIS HIPS against Josie's bottom as he came. "I'm coming. God, I'm coming." Again, he pumped into her, and then again as he filled her and let out a long, deep growl of satisfaction.

His cock struck her tender G-spot as he throbbed, and she climaxed again with a shudder, leaning against her forearm, which was pressed against the tiled wall of the shower. That made three orgasms for her in fifteen minutes. Josie was a female lost to her hormones, and Tristan wasn't complaining. In the past week, they had fucked ten ways to Sunday. In the shower, on the kitchen counter, on the couch, in bed, on the floor, on the dining room table. She couldn't get enough, and Tristan aimed to please, eager to ride out the sexual roller coaster with her.

"You've been insatiable, baby," he said quietly against her shoulder, breathless and still waxing in the afterglow of hot and dirty shower sex.

"Hormones," she said, just as out of breath as he was. "They do a girl's body good."

"They do my body good, too."

She huffed a gentle laugh. "Is that so?"

"Mm-hm." He nibbled her neck, groaning through a tiny aftershock as she sighed. After several more luxurious seconds within her swollen warmth, he slid himself out and rinsed them both off.

"You hungry?" She turned and slung her arms lazily over his shoulders.

"I could eat." He kissed her full lips.

"I'll go fix you an egg salad sandwich while you finish up." She kissed him back and stepped out of the shower.

"Don't exert yourself." Tristan reached for the shampoo as he watched her wrap a towel around her slim body. Within a couple of months, her belly would swell with his child. Already, she had gained three pounds as her appetite increased.

She flashed him a curious glance over her shoulder and laughed. "Exert myself? Making an egg salad sandwich?"

Chagrined, Tristan rolled his eyes at himself. "I know, I know. I'm sorry. I just want you to take it easy." He was already becoming protective of her and the baby. Overly so. He didn't want her trying to do too much. She should lie down and rest more. They had been given a gift, and he didn't want to leave anything to chance.

"Baby, I'll be fine. Stop worrying about me." She blew him another kiss as she hurried out of the bathroom to prevent cool air from rushing in, and he returned to his shower, which she had interrupted within a minute of him starting it. But she could interrupt all she wanted if the result was as hot as their interlude had just been. If what he'd gone through with Josie in the past week was even a fraction of what happened to a male in his *calling*, Tristan was jealous of mated males. Damn, he could get used to this nonstop sex thing.

A few minutes later, Tristan shut off the shower, dried off, and slipped into sweats and a T-shirt, then made his way to the kitchen.

"Oh my God," Josie spun for the sink just as Tristan walked around the corner.

"Baby? You o—"

She bent over and vomited into the sink...just let loose without so much as a warning.

Tristan rushed to her side and smoothed his hand over her back as she continued to throw up. "Josie? You okay? Just breathe, baby." Morning sickness. Had to be. Let the bad part about being pregnant begin.

Her body convulsed through another spasm, and then finally it was over. Tristan turned on the faucet to rinse out the sink, and he quickly grabbed a glass and filled it with water, then held it out to her as she stood and wiped her mouth with a trembling hand.

"You okay?" he said again.

She nodded, took the water, and sipped. "Yeah. I think so." She took a deep breath and glanced toward the opposite counter. "I took the lid off the egg salad, and as soon as I smelled it…" She fought back a gag.

Tristan hurriedly put the lid back on the container and shoved it back in the fridge. "Maybe roast beef will be safer." He smiled over his shoulder at her, and she nodded.

"Yes. Much safer."

She started to take the roast beef from him, but still looked green around the gills. Tristan squeezed her hand. "I can manage. Why don't you just sit down? I'll make you some tea."

With a grateful nod, she turned and took a seat at the table. "Good idea."

He filled the teakettle with water and set it on the stove. "Looks like we've hit the fun part."

"What? The part where I puke my guts out every day?" She settled in the chair, arm over her stomach. She still looked queasy.

He gave her a sympathetic smile. "I hope it won't be that bad."

She waved him off. "It's okay. If this is what I have to go through to have the miracle baby"—she smiled and patted her tummy—"then I guess that's what I'll have to do."

"Only you would make a joke at a time like this."

"It's why you love me," she said with a wink. "My twisted sense of humor."

As the water heated, he turned his attention to putting together his sandwich. "That's only one reason why I love you," he said, and then licked mustard off his thumb.

"How many reasons are there?"

The lighthearted banter felt nice. Comfortable. Right in so many ways. He relished these quiet, easy moments between them.

"About a thousand." He grabbed a tea bag and plopped it in a cup before pouring hot water over it.

"Only a thousand?" she said, teasing him.

He set her mug in front of her with a spoon. "Give or take."

Their eyes met and held for a long moment as unspoken love filled the quiet space, and then Tristan bent down, brushed his lips over hers, and smiled against her mouth. "I love you to infinity, baby."

"Ditto," she said, combing her fingers through his hair.

He leaned in to the caress. "I'll take care of you through this."

"You don't need—"

He held up his hand. "No, Josie. Let me do my duty. As the male, it's my responsibility to tend to you while you're pregnant." He turned his face to her palm and kissed it. "If you're sick, it's my job to stay with you, ease your discomfort, and take care of you."

Her expression relaxed, and understanding filled her eyes. She knew how badly he wanted to be mated to her. Really, officially, bound-by-the-king's-law mated. He had told her so countless times. And a true mate, bound by biology and tethered soul-to-soul by a link so powerful it could kill a male if broken, would tend to his female while she was pregnant. He would hold her hair out of her face as she got sick. He would gently wipe her mouth after. He would make her tea, feed her, bathe her, wash her hair, and massage her feet. Whatever it took to keep her comfortable and as happy as possible. That was his job.

"Okay," she said with a gentle nod. "I'd love that."

He kissed her again, returned to the kitchen for his sandwich, and rejoined her at the table as she stirred sugar into her tea. "Better?" he asked as she sipped.

"I think it's passed," she said.

Seeing her sick like that had momentarily worried him before his instinct to take care of her kicked in.

"My team got invited to the king's holiday party this year. Should I cancel?"

Josie cocked her head to the side. "Why? Because I might have morning sickness? Hell no. It's been three years since we were able to attend King Bain's Christmas party. I wouldn't miss that for anything."

"You sure?"

"Positive."

Tristan chuckled. "You're such a tough little thing."

"Well, I'm mated to you. I have to be."

He looked down at his sandwich. "Technically, you're not mated—"

"Tristan." Her voice held a warning tone. "I know how I feel. And whether we're connected biologically or not, you're my mate and I'm yours."

Her getting pregnant had awakened all his old fears. What if someone else came along who mated her? Or what if he mated to another? He couldn't bear the thought of losing her simply because his DNA hadn't gotten with the program to connect him to her forever.

"Tristan, look at me," she said, her tone commanding.

He met her gaze.

"We're mates, Tristan," she said. "In my heart, I know it. Just because that whole vampire biological hocus-pocus didn't magically activate between us doesn't make us any less mates."

He took her hand and lifted it to his lips. "I know. I just want...I feel..." He closed his eyes. "I'm afraid of losing you."

"You won't lose me." Her fingers opened and caressed his cheek. "Never."

He nodded again and kissed her palm. "Never," he whispered against her skin. "You're mine." As he said it, he meant it. Josie belonged to him. And if anything happened to take her away from him, he knew it would kill him.

CHAPTER 8

CHRISTMAS EVE

King Bain loved watching Cara get ready for parties. She moved with the elegant grace fitting for a queen, her long fingers plucking a broach from a velvet-lined chest on her dressing table, her back straight yet relaxed.

Her kind, blue eyes met his in the mirror. "I'm hurrying," she said.

He grinned and pushed away from the wall where he'd parked moments ago, arms crossed. "I'm not rushing you. I'm admiring you." He knelt behind her and skimmed one hand around her slender waist. "There's a difference."

"I certainly hope so." She grinned coquettishly as she pinned the ruby and diamond broach in the center of the velvet bodice of her off-the-shoulder gown. "But didn't you admire me enough earlier?"

"Mmm." Bain slid his other arm around her waist and kissed the back of her shoulder. "Not nearly enough, my queen. And I plan on admiring you again after the party. After I get you out of this lovely dress." In addition to the velvet bodice, the burgundy gown draped into layers of chiffon skirting and came with a matching wrap. The dark color accented Cara's olive complexion and black hair perfectly.

Cara leaned into his embrace. "You do dote on me."

He peppered kisses along the back of her neck, under her upswept hair. "It's my duty to dote."

Her fingers slid into his long hair as she tipped her head forward. "You're good at your duty."

If he didn't stop, they wouldn't make it downstairs in time to greet their guests, so he slowly pulled away and took a seat beside her dressing table so he could watch her put on the finishing touches of her makeup.

"You know, my next *calling* is due in a year or so," he said as he ran a fingertip up her arm. "Can we talk about it?"

It had been almost three decades since his second child, Colin, had been born, and he was ready for another. Like humans, vampires could use contraceptives to prevent pregnancy, and Cara had used them during his last two *calling* phases. He would prefer not to use them during his next.

Cara stiffened. "You know how hard Colin's birth was on me."

"Yes, but Miriam's wasn't." Miriam was their firstborn. She had been easy to birth, but was turning out to be hell to raise. She was so damned spirited and rebellious as of late. Even so, Bain longed for another child. It was the way of the mated male, to always yearn for young.

Cara bowed her head. "I know. I'm just worried. I don't think I can take another birth like Colin's."

For starters, morning sickness had lasted all nine months of Cara's pregnancy with Colin. And when the time came to give birth, Colin presented breech. The doctors had had to turn him inside the womb, which had been a nightmare for Cara. She had refused a Cesarean delivery. And then Colin got stubborn and wouldn't budge. Labor had lasted nearly two days, and Cara had been beyond exhausted when she finally squeezed him out.

"I want another child, Cara," Bain said as delicately as possible. He had failed with Miriam and Colin on so many levels, a point he was becoming clearer on as Miriam approached the age of official vampire adulthood. For humans, eighteen was when kids became adults. For vampires, sixty was the official age of adulthood, even though many mated before reaching that age. Miriam was forty-seven, but behaved like an adolescent human emotionally more often than not. She was so bright. So educated and cunning. And yet, she was often quarrelsome and behaved mutinously against his household rules, slipping away with her friends without permission, arguing with him over such silly trifles as what clothes she could and could not wear and when.

If he could have another child, he could prove to himself that he could be a better father than he had been to Miriam and Colin. This was essential to him.

Cara set down her lipstick with a sigh then turned a compassionate smile on him. "Okay, we can talk about it. I know this is important to you."

Relieved that she seemed open to the subject, Bain settled back in his chair.

She returned to applying her makeup and primping. "Speaking of children, Miriam is upset she doesn't get to attend tonight's party."

Bain bristled. Miriam was becoming more and more rebellious and headstrong in recent months. Like a human fifteen-year-old, she wanted to be an adult when she wasn't yet emotionally ready.

Miriam wasn't just any old random vampire. She was the princess. His enemies could use her to get to him. They could hurt her to hurt him. He had put rules in place to protect her, but she didn't understand them. She thought he was being overly protective, and in a way he was. Those rules were meant to keep her safe and even save her life, as well the lives of the entire royal family.

And tonight's party was not the place for her to lose sight of her role.

He stood and paced away. "She'll understand."

Cara turned to face him and placed her hands in her lap. "Maybe you should reconsider."

Bain frowned at her. "What?"

She nodded her head to the side as if to tell him to hear her out. "Bain, she's restless. What would be the harm?"

"The harm is that this party isn't a controlled environment." He was very careful about the males he put in front of Miriam. She was a beautiful female, and Bain wasn't stupid. Anything could happen when he had all walks of life in attendance, and Bain wouldn't risk that one of those males would form an improper relationship with his daughter.

Cara sighed impatiently. "Well, let's talk about that, Bain," she said. "Gregos's son, Arion, will be there. Arion is a worthy, respectable male, isn't he? What if he's the one meant to mate Miriam? You've been parading male after male in front of her for years, hoping that one would form a mating bond to her, but none have. Maybe Arion's the one. Wouldn't that be something?"

Bain shook his head. "And Arion's best friend is that philandering, womanizing jackass, Io. He'll be at the party, too. He's not the kind of male I want around my daughter, Cara. And she's become so rebellious lately that she probably wouldn't hesitate to run off with that Casanova just to spite me."

"Bain." Cara sighed heavily. "You can't protect her forever."

"I know I can't, but I can try."

"Then why did you buy her a car for Christmas?" Cara said, voice raised. "If you're so worried about her getting into trouble, isn't a car the worst thing you can buy her? To send her out into the world where she can get in trouble?"

"She won't be allowed to leave without an armed escort. She'll be guarded. And I'll be able to track her."

Cara shook her head. "You're going to push her further away, Bain. You know she won't want to be guarded twenty-four-seven. She's too stubborn. She has too much of you in her."

"She'll understand when she gets older."

"Will she?"

"What's that supposed to mean?" Bain said. "Of course she will. I will stop at nothing to keep my children safe. There are too many people out there who would use them to hurt me. I can't let that happen."

Cara stared blankly at him for a moment then stood. "And you want to talk to me about having another child?" Her words and the critical tone of her voice stunned him. "Bain," she said, "until you realize you can't treat your children this way, threat or not, I'm not sure having another child is a good idea." She grabbed her pocketbook from the foot of the bed. "Maybe you need to think about that before we discuss your next *calling*. I'll wait for you in the hall." Sweeping her skirt away from her feet, Cara turned and left the room.

Bain stared after her, too frustrated to move. He knew what was best for his daughter, and he would do whatever it took to keep her safe. And tonight that included not allowing her to attend the party. End of discussion.

But he still wanted another child. That part of the conversation wasn't over.

TRISTAN SAT ON THE COUCH in his midnight-blue, three-piece suit. The red silk tie and jacquard vest lent a festive spirit to the otherwise stuffy attire. The sound of the bedroom door closing down the hall brought his expectant gaze up to the hallway. A moment later, Josie appeared, wrapped in shimmering red satin, her breasts pushed invitingly into perfect, pristine mounds above the angular, off-the-shoulder neckline.

"You look..."

"Beautiful?" Josie suggested flirtatiously.

Tristan shook his head as he rose. "Radiant."

Her rouged cheeks lifted as her matte red lips broke into a smile.

"Red has always been your color, baby." Tristan slipped his arm around her waist and kissed her cheek. "How do you feel?"

"Good for now." She patted her stomach.

She hadn't suffered any morning sickness all day, so hopefully they would make it through the party. Tristan knew how much Josie looked forward to these rare social occasions.

"You ready?" he said, reaching for her faux fur coat. They could afford the real thing, but Josie insisted on buying fakes. She was too much of an animal lover to wear them as clothes.

Just as he was easing her coat over her shoulders, his phone rang. He pulled it out of his breast pocket and frowned.

"Who is it?" Josie said, adjusting her sleeves.

"AKM Dispatch." He connected the call. "Yeah, this is Tristan."

"I'm sorry, Tristan," the dispatcher said, "but we have an emergency."

"I'm on my way out the door for the king's par—"

"I understand, but this is urgent. We just received a report of three mutants on the South Side."

Mutants? Three of them? At the same time? That was too much for the two teams on duty to handle. What happened to Christmas Eve being traditionally slow? "I'll be right there. Call in my team."

Josie's forehead crinkled with dismay. "What's wrong? Why aren't we going to the party?"

He disconnected the call and hurried for the bedroom. "Mutants. Three of them," he said over his shoulder. "And we'll still go to the party. We'll just be a little late."

"But...?" Josie hesitated in the doorway as Tristan stripped out of his suit.

"I know. I'm sorry, baby. This will only take a couple of hours at most. I swear." Tristan stopped and took her face in his hands, kissed her, and gazed into those gorgeous, multi-hued eyes of hers. "We'll go. I promise. I won't let you miss the king's Christmas party."

Smiling, she gave a resigned nod before smiling. "I know. It's your job. This is all part of being mated to an enforcer."

After giving her another quick kiss, Tristan hurried into the closet, pulled on his pseudo-military gear, and then grabbed his work coat. Josie was in the living room, sitting on the couch, flipping through channels on the television.

"I'll be back as soon as I can," he said, sweeping in to kiss her cheek.

"I'll be waiting." She blinked up at him, her eyes full of love.

Josie never argued with him over his job. She understood that he couldn't always be there when she wanted him to be. And yet, she took everything like a trooper, smile and all.

"See you soon." He hurried for the door as she blew him a kiss.

It took him all of five minutes to get downstairs from his on-site apartment to the main floor and into the war room. By the time the first members of his team arrived fifteen minutes later, he had been briefed on the situation. Three mutants. Stryker's team had corralled them inside an abandoned warehouse on the South Side. At least this way, the mutants wouldn't pose more of a threat than they already had to both the human and vampire populations. Mutants were the deadliest creatures known and only came into being when a vampire—usually a mixed-blood—lost control of his or her inborn, genetic powers. The transition could take days or even weeks, which made the fact that they had three of them in one place at the same time a little hard to believe.

Ari and Io burst into the war room, still strapping on gear. Malek appeared a few seconds later.

"Where's Micah and Trace?" Tristan said, securing iron braces around his forearms. The others already had theirs on, which were standard attire when fighting a mutant, along with iron collars and chest plates. Shit, they should have just geared up in head-to-toe armor. One bite from a mutant meant *sayonara baby*. Their venom was too poisonous for even vampires to heal from.

Malek, Ari, and Io looked at each other and shrugged. "We haven't seen them," Malek said.

A quick check with Dispatch revealed that neither had answered their mobiles.

Great. They were two men down and going into a fight with mutants.

Tristan checked his watch then eyed the second team preparing to dematerialize to the scene. Mutant calls were too urgent to mess with driving. You either vapored to the action or you didn't go at all.

"We'll have to go without them." Tristan chambered a special mercury-tipped round in his Glock. Everything about taking down a mutant was special, from the armor, to the mode of travel, to the specially made bullets required to kill them. Regular bullets would slow a mutant down, but they wouldn't kill them. They needed mercury for that. Certain types of acid worked, too. "Who's got the cartridges for Stryker's team?"

Io lifted the bag he was holding. "Got 'em."

"Okay. Let's go." Tristan hurried out of the weapons room, his team on his heels.

Once they reached what they called the vapor room, where enforcers mobilized to dematerialize, Tristan looked over his shoulder. "Follow my trail." With that, he closed his eyes, exhaled, and turned to mist.

Within seconds, he reappeared at the abandoned warehouse. Shrieks ripped the air from the trapped mutants.

"Fuck me!" Ari said from behind him.

Gunshots rang out, followed by shouting from members of Stryker's team.

"Io!" Tristan snapped his fingers. "Get those cartridges to those men. Now! Ari, go with him."

In a flash of supernatural speed both would feel later when their adrenaline came down, Ari and Io disappeared into the melee.

"Malek, come with me." Tristan and Malek had known each other since the reign of King Bain the First, over eight hundred years. They meshed well on the battlefield, cuing in to each other seamlessly.

Like joined shadows, he and Malek darted wordlessly into the warehouse. It was dark inside, but his hunting sight was better than night vision glasses, and he easily worked his way through the maze of abandoned furniture and empty offices.

As he sidestepped through a jumble of half-full boxes, which held everything from abandoned office supplies to bits and pieces of mechanical scrap, he stubbed the boot of his toe on a metal rod "Fuck," he bit out as the rod slid down the wall and fell to the concrete floor with a clang.

More shouting came at him from inside the guts of the warehouse, followed by more gunshots. A bullet broke through the plaster wall and whizzed between him and Malek, embedding into the outside wall. Malek jerked backward and cursed as he ducked.

"Shit!" Tristan spun and met Malek's startled gaze. "Let's go!"

They took off at a run, and a moment later, they busted through a door that led into the cavernous space that had, at one time, been used to store pallets of materials, but which now lay like a wasteland, with only more abandoned boxes of scrap scattered here and there. Industrial metal shelves extended from floor to ceiling in rows along one wall, creating perfect hiding places.

A shadow blurred by in a flash of movement, and Tristan jumped back against Malek before pulling himself together and taking off after it. Malek's pounding footfalls let Tristan know his buddy was on him like glue.

The inky humanoid shadow slowed then stopped, then morphed into a solid, dark mass as it turned to face him and Malek. Yellow, red-rimmed irises beamed malevolently at Tristan as a beastly screech split the air. Meet mutant number one, and even though it was hunched over, Tristan could tell it was a big fucker. Saliva dripped from its misshapen mouth.

Tristan skidded to a stop, lifted his Glock, and fired.

The mutant ricocheted back as the bullet plowed into its left shoulder. Another animalistic shrill pierced the night as the mutant threw its head back and howled.

"Fuck, it's big," Malek said beside him.

"And pissed off." Tristan took aim again, but the mutant snarled and leaped away before he could get off another round. "Goddammit!"

"Follow it!" With his gun raised, Malek took off, eyes searching.

The iron guards adorning Tristan's body cut into his skin as he beat feet with Malek to follow the mutant's trail, but it had disappeared. Damn bastard. Where had it gone?

As he and Malek met back-to-back and slowly turned in a coordinated circle, guns raised toward the tops of the towering shelves, Stryker and Luca—a member of his team—

charged around a nearby corner and almost ran into them.

Tristan and Malek separated.

"Where is it?" Stryker barked. He was full-on military badass. Stryker would have made one hell of a Marine had he been human.

"I don't know, but I hit it once in the shoulder. It should be slowing down wherever it is." Tristan lowered his gun and glanced around the darkness and up toward the ceiling. "Where are the other two?"

Stryker pointed back the way he'd come. "Other side of the warehouse."

"You don't have armor," Tristan said, frowning at Stryker's and Luca's exposed arms and necks.

"No time to put it on." Stryker glared into the darkness.

Stryker's team had been on patrol tonight, and each enforcer's vehicle was loaded with mutant armor. But if Stryker said he didn't have time, he didn't have time. The guy wasn't prone to recklessness or lying.

"How the hell did we get three of these fuckers in one night?" Tristan said as the four turned in place and kept their eyes on the shadows.

"Hell if I know," Stryker glared toward the tops of the shelves. "We found their shredded clothes a few blocks away, tracked them, and corralled them here until you sunshiny people arrived."

"Anything useful in the clothes?" Malek said, gun raised, eyes alert.

"I'm not sure." Stryker's eyes narrowed as he looked toward the ceiling. "All three had cobalt paraphernalia on them."

"Cobalt?" Tristan frowned. "They were all cobalt users?" That couldn't just be coincidence.

Stryker nodded. "Yep, from the looks of it, they—fuck! Look out!"

A black mist vaulted off the top of a nearby shelf, landing in the middle of their small circle. The four of them scampered away, guns up.

"Malek! Over here!" Tristan didn't want Malek in the line of fire.

The impressive behemoth formed from the vapor, shot its lethal gaze toward Luca, who was the closest, and lunged. Stryker reached for Luca to pull him out of the way, but the mutant moved faster than he did, latched onto Luca, sank its mutated fangs into his upper arm, and dragged him off in a blink before they could even lift their weapons.

"NO!" Stryker gave chase, and Tristan and Malek brought up the rear, running back into the heart of the warehouse.

Luca's cries for help echoed through the open space like a rubber ball bouncing off the walls, then suddenly turned into screams of horror.

"No! No! NOOOO!" Luca's voice fell into unintelligible, blood-drenched syllables, and Tristan, Stryker, and Malek leaped in two bounds to the top of the industrial shelves where the mutant had taken his prey.

The beast let go of Luca long enough to swing its gaze around to the three of them with their guns trained on its head and torso. Angry gurgles bubbled inside the mutant's throat. The mercury from Tristan's earlier shot was slowly corroding the creature's blood vessels, but not fast enough. Beneath its gnarled claws, Luca screamed and thrashed as poison broke through his system. Mutant venom was nothing like vampire venom. Where vampire venom created a pleasurable euphoria in one who was bitten, mutant venom created the opposite. Agonizing and brutal, mutant venom sent its victims into an ugly, ferocious death. No one wanted to die from a mutant's bite.

The mutant rose to its hind legs and growled.

"Shoot it!" Tristan aimed and fired. Malek and Stryker did likewise, and a cacophony of gunshots echoed off the walls.

Their bullets struck the mutant's body, splattering rotting flesh and black blood. Its unhinged jaw opened wide as the creature screamed and staggered backward, tripped over Luca's body, and fell to the dirty, cement floor. Already, the mutant's young body had begun to twist and metamorphose into a quadruped. Its back was hunched and resembled that of a werewolf, and its arms were longer and more muscular, its face more elongated. Within hours, it likely would have been roaming on all fours, scouring the streets for victims.

Tristan and the others, out of breath, looked down at the creature but kept their guns raised until it became clear the damn thing wasn't going anywhere. Blood oozed from numerous bullet wounds, and its long, craggy fingers curled like claws as if it were still trying to shred Luca apart. In a couple more minutes, the mutant would be nothing but a carcass.

Luca.

Tristan turned as Stryker rushed forward and fell to his knees at Luca's side.

"Fuck!" Stryker cursed and holstered his weapon. "God, I'm sorry, Luca. I'm so sorry."

Luca shivered violently, his teeth chattering so hard it was a wonder they didn't chip. His skin was already turning black, the whites of his eyes filling with blood. His organs were dissolving. Mutant venom was like Ebola for vampires, only faster. What took Ebola weeks to accomplish with humans took only minutes for vampires. At least mutant venom didn't create a contagion in its host. That was the only reprieve. That and the swiftness by which it killed. Even so, it was a wretched, painful way to die.

Tristan and Malek could only look on as Stryker held Luca's hand in his final minutes. They were helpless to stop the disintegration. Their scientists had never been able to develop an antidote for mutant venom, because it was as unique as its host. To develop an antidote, a sample of each vampire's venom would have to be taken and a unique antidote made for each, which was impossible. How would you track such a serum? Store it? And how long would it remain effective?

So all they could do was handle mutants case-by-case as they had done tonight.

"Tell...Mazie...I...love her." Every hoarse, whispered word was a labor for Luca to speak.

"I will." Stryker clamped both hands around Luca's. "I'll make sure they're taken care of."

Luca blinked and shuddered. "Thank...you."

Tristan turned away out of respect as Luca drew his final breaths, and then it was over. Luca was gone, and so was the mutant.

Stryker sighed in frustrated sorrow, and then slowly stood before radioing the rest of his team. "Status?"

Bauer's voice came back through the radio. "Two mutants down here. Bagging them now."

"Casualties?" Stryker asked.

"None as far as I can tell."

Stryker glanced down at Luca's body, and then exchanged looks with Tristan before hitting his mic and saying, "One down here. We'll need to inform Luca's family."

Silence. Then, "Roger that." A curse broke through the static before Bauer turned off his mic.

Stryker hung his head briefly then turned toward Tristan. "Help me carry him out?"

Tristan stepped forward. "Of course." He turned to Malek then nodded toward the dead mutant on the floor. "Let's bag it up."

Twenty minutes later, they loaded the dead mutants in the back of Stryker's black AKM Suburban. Luca's body was carefully wrapped in white linen and placed in the back of Bauer's vehicle.

"I'll see you at the party later," Tristan said to Malek.

"You're not coming back with us?"

Tristan shook his head. "No. I'm going to ride in with Stryker." He didn't want to leave Stryker alone right now. As a fellow team leader, Tristan understood what it was like to lose a member of the team. Tristan had lost a couple over the years, but this was Stryker's first. Besides, he wanted to see if he could get more information about what had happened tonight. Three mutants in one night? At the same time, no less? That was a bit too coincidental. Could there be a connection to the cobalt? It was a stretch, but all three had been using the dreck-made drug.

Malek, Ari, and Io vapored back home, and Tristan hopped in the passenger seat of Stryker's SUV. "All set," he said quietly.

Stryker lifted his head and nodded. He didn't look so good. Angry. Pissed off. Upset. Sad. His expression was a stew of emotions.

"You want me to drive?" Tristan motioned toward the steering wheel.

Stryker shook his head tightly. "I'm good." He put the Suburban in gear, turned the vehicle around, and headed toward AKM.

"So, tell me about tonight," Tristan said. "What happened?"

Stryker cleared his throat and kept his heavy gaze aimed out the windshield. "Bauer took a call about cobalt activity in the area, so he and Luca came to check it out."

"Did they find anything?"

Stryker shook his head. "By the time they arrived, the dealers were gone."

"Then what?"

Stryker stopped at a red light and glanced at Tristan. "As they were looking around the area, they found shredded clothes. First it was just one set, then they found another, and then a third."

Shredded clothes were always the first sign of the birth of a mutant, whose body swelled as chemical reactions broke at an accelerated rate within its cells, which enlarged by at least fifty percent, sometimes even bigger. From the look of tonight's mutants, they were facing the "even bigger" side of the scale.

After taking a deep breath, Stryker continued. "The entire team was called in at that point, and we quickly corralled the mutants inside that warehouse and called for backup. Had to wipe a few humans who got stuck in the crosshairs."

"And you went in without armor?"

Stryker frowned. "We couldn't risk them getting out into the human population."

Tristan raised his hands. "Hey, I'm not judging. I'm just trying to put the pieces together."

Stryker's expression eased and he rolled his eyes. "Who am I kidding? Going in without armor was stupid." He hit the steering wheel with his right hand. "Fuck! I never should have let Luca go in like that. I shouldn't have risked it."

Tristan glanced out the passenger window then looked back across the seat. "You can't go back and change it, Stryke. It's done. Don't beat yourself up over this. We all make these life-and-death decisions. Most of the time, they're the right ones, and sometimes, even when they're right, bad things happen. Luca knew the risks. We all do. They're part of the job."

"Tell that to his mate," Stryker said quietly.

Tristan didn't envy Stryker's responsibility to tell Luca's mate that he was dead. It was a responsibility they each took on as team leaders. For all Stryker's military bravado and hard, ice-cold exterior, the guy had a warm heart. For the first time, Tristan was getting a look at a Stryker he had never known. A Stryker full of doubt, who might even be questioning his role as an enforcement team leader. A Stryker whose guard was briefly down. Tristan wasn't used to seeing his comrade in such a state. Then again, the death of a team member could bring out the worst in a person.

"Do you think cobalt did this?" A change of subject might be good, and Tristan was curious to see if Stryker felt the same way he did about the cobalt connection.

Stryker shrugged as he made a left turn. "I don't know. It's damn ironic that all three had recently been using, though, if you ask me. Or maybe it's just coincidence. They were all mixed-bloods, according to their IDs."

Mixed-bloods were more prone to going mutant than full-bloods, but Tristan didn't believe in coincidences. "I'm not buying it." He glowered out the window.

"Neither am I, but there's nothing solid to connect the cobalt to them going mutant, Tris. Lots of vampires use cobalt, and this is the first time we've seen users go beast like that."

What Stryker said was true, but still, Tristan couldn't shake the feeling that somehow there was a connection. For now, he would have to set his concerns aside. Until he had hard evidence, there wasn't much he or anyone else could do to accuse the drecks of using cobalt as a weapon to kill vampires. Besides, he had a pretty lady in red at home who was eager to get to the social event of the season. For the rest of the night, Josie had to be his primary concern. He had promised her the king's party, and he would make good on his promise.

The drecks and their potential cobalt-mutant connection would have to wait.

Deacon pulled out his mobile and hit Bishop's speed dial.

"Yes?" Bishop's voice oozed through the connection.

"It worked."

"Oh?" Bishop perked up. "Tell me more, brother."

Deacon peered into the darkness as if making sure no one else was around. "Within seconds of shooting up, the three mongrels began to turn. It was quite marvelous to watch. From a distance, of course." He chuckled. "And Bain's enforcers had quite a fight on their hands. You'll be pleased to hear that one was killed."

"Aaawwe, how unfortunate for Bain's men. Remind me to send my condolences." Bishop's voice held the sinister sarcasm he usually reverted to when talking about Bain and his legion of vampires.

Deacon smiled. "So, all in all, it was a good night, wouldn't you say? Four down, thousands to go."

"Agreed, but...hmmm." Bishop sounded reticent. "The reaction was too fast. I don't want them turning so soon after doping. I don't want to risk Bain's prattling dolts making the connection between cobalt and their savage, miscreant mutants."

"I agree." Deacon turned on the roof he'd remained stationed on during the battle below and began heading off. "But at least we know we're on the right course."

"Yes, that's true. In that regard, it *was* a successful field test." Bishop sounded thoughtful. "And Apostle is unaware of your presence?"

Deacon nodded as he opened the door that led from the

roof to a utility room and down a flight of rickety, metal stairs. "Yes." Deacon's twin ran the show in Chicago, as well as elsewhere, but not even Apostle knew just how deep Deacon and Bishop's experiments ran. Not yet. In time, they would loop him in. Once the formula was mastered. All Apostle needed to know right now was that they needed him to find as many drug-using vamps as he could.

"Good. Return at once, brother. I want to begin tweaking the formula immediately. Pick up from Lorena, first, though. She has two subjects in her possession."

"Of course." Deacon disconnected, descended the long metal staircase in the abandoned building, slid out the back, trekked in the shadows several blocks to his rented SUV, and then disappeared into the night.

CHAPTER 9

KING BAIN WORKED HIS WAY THROUGH THE SCORES of dignitaries, liaisons, counselors, and VIPs gathered in the ballroom. This wasn't his home—because only a select few were allowed inside his residence—but he kept an elegantly appointed off-residence judicial building, which doubled as a gathering place for social events like his annual Christmas party.

Red and green damask screens hung in lustrous waves from the ceiling to the floor between large picture windows, which were adorned with white, gauzy sheers that resembled snow. In the corner stood a giant Christmas tree, decorated in red, gold, green, and silver. Twinkle lights blinked from within the garland, and a handmade crystal star sat atop the tree like a delicate beacon. A variety of candlelit cocktail tables dotted the space around the bar. Generous, round banquet tables with impeccable, gold and crystal place settings commanded half the room, and a twelve-piece orchestra played festive holiday music near the area set aside for dancing.

The décor was certainly fit for a king, as well as for a party.

Cara settled into the circle of his arm as he guided her from one guest to another, exchanging pleasantries and seasonal wishes, but concern worried his mind. His enforcers had been dispatched on a multi-mutant call tonight, which had detained some of his guests.

Three mutants together, all at once, alarmed him. Chicago hadn't seen a mutant in months, and now, just like that on Christmas Eve, three. It didn't make sense.

From across the room, Bain saw Gregos's son Arion enter,

dressed exquisitely in a black, three-piece suit and red tie.

"Arion, what a pleasure to see you again," Bain said after separating from Cara and working his way through the crowd.

"The pleasure is mine." Arion bowed, always the picture of propriety. Arion's father was one of Bain's most trusted liaisons, with ancient bloodlines and an immaculate pedigree. He expected nothing less than precision and perfection from the son of Gregos.

Bain could only be so lucky to have Arion mate his daughter, as Cara had suggested. Perhaps he would arrange a meeting after all, to see if the proverbial sparks flew between Arion and Miriam. Enforcers weren't the typical match Bain tried to present to Miriam, but for Arion, he could make an exception.

Io, Tristan, and Josie entered the Great Hall and joined them.

"Josie, you look radiant." Bain smiled but forced back the subtle ache in his heart. "I heard the good news that you're expecting. Congratulations." He forced his façade not to crack under the weight of his personal feelings. The fact that he wanted another child of his own during his next *calling* was not cause to be jealous of Josie and Tristan's good fortune. They deserved his generous felicitations, as would anyone in their position.

"Thank you." She curtsied and snuggled into Tristan's embrace almost shyly, which was a characteristic he wasn't used to seeing in Josie. She was usually such a strong personality, but then, pregnancy had a way of making females behave in ways out of character from their normal proclivities.

Bain extended his hand to Tristan. "Congratulations, my friend."

Tristan nodded proudly. "Thank you. It was a surprise to be sure." He glanced down at Josie with love in his eyes.

"Ah, yes." Bain grinned magnanimously. "I can imagine."

Bain knew the mated status of everyone within his inner circle, as well as most within his middle circle, and he knew Tristan had never actually mated Josie. As the king, he presided over the legal proceedings and handled the decrees regarding such matters. Vampire mates didn't necessarily hold marriage ceremonies, but a male did have to file an order with the royal counsel to ensure legal recognition of his mated status once he took a mate. Really, though, even that was merely a technicality. If a mated male could prove a female was his mate, which wasn't hard to do, Bain's laws recognized him accordingly even if no mating order had been filed. Vampire law was very lenient toward the rights of mated males, given that the repercussions of denying a mated male were so severe.

Tristan had never filed such an order, and he didn't display mated tendencies, which included extreme aggression and severe possessiveness of his female. The fact that Josie was with his child was a few prayers short of a miracle.

Io and Arion slipped away into the crowd as Malek arrived and joined them, which left Bain with Tristan and Josie.

"I heard about what happened tonight," Bain said.

Tristan's expression grew grim. "Yes. It was..."

"Concerning." Bain paused and bowed his head. "And tragic."

Josie huddled a little closer to Tristan and wrapped her arm around his waist.

Losing an enforcer always sucked the air out of life for all involved. Each of Bain's men took the loss personally, as did he. And what of Luca's family? Of course, Bain would see to it that they were provided for, but he couldn't replace the loss of a loved one. He couldn't bring Luca back from the dead, and that was what his mate really needed more than anything.

After a moment's silence, Bain cleared his throat, glanced up, and looked around. "So, where's Micah?"

Tristan shrugged. "I don't know. He didn't show for the call tonight, either."

This was not good news. Bain had heard about Micah's relationship woes and that things weren't going well. He had held high hopes that the relationship would succeed and that Micah would return to his old self...the shrewd, skilled warrior he had been almost a millennium ago.

"And no one's heard from him?" Bain's jaw tightened.

Tristan shook his head. "No. Nothing. And no one's heard from Trace, either."

Bain frowned and looked away. Trace was the quiet one. The mysterious one who spoke only when it was necessary, and then usually only one syllable at a time. But Trace was solid, never a troublemaker. Until now. From what he knew of Trace's record, it wasn't like him to not answer a call or at least check in.

"Keep me posted," Bain said. "I worry about Micah."

"I do, too," Tristan said.

Josie spoke up. "So do I." She sounded more concerned than they did.

The three exchanged uneasy glances, and then Bain took a spirited breath and blew it sharply out. "Well, let's not be somber tonight." He gestured toward the tree. "This is supposed to be a happy occasion. There will be plenty of time after the holiday to mourn. For tonight, let's try to be happy." He waved toward the banquet tables. "We'll be having a meal fit for a king soon." Bain forced a smile. "So eat, drink, be merry." Then he leaned close to them and said, "And think good thoughts for our friend Micah, as well as for our lost comrade."

Tristan nodded and smiled, as did Josie. "Yes. Good thoughts."

"Enjoy yourselves tonight." With a wink, Bain bowed his head so that his long, black hair fell off his shoulders. Then he rose back to his full height, turned, and made his way back to Cara.

Despite his words of good cheer, a heaviness fell over his heart. Too much sorrow surrounded the evening. Luca's death. Now Micah. Where was his old friend? Bain's instincts told him something bad had happened. Bain only hoped that Micah had the strength to survive it. Micah wasn't like other vampires. He was special, and right now, that might be his only saving grace if what Bain thought had happened had come to pass. If his relationship with Jackson had come to an end, Micah would need every bit of what made him special to survive, especially after how he reacted to Katarina's death. God help him.

Across town, Micah sat on his balcony in his suit, alone, cold, and still as stone. He had been there for hours, freezing but unfeeling, ignoring the incessant ringing of his phone, abandoning reality as heartache and suffering seeped into his heart. There would be no holiday party for him. No more happiness. No more life. Jackson was gone.

In truth, he had been gone for weeks. But tonight, Jackson had made it final. He had broken up with Micah. On Christmas Eve. Merry Fucking Christmas to him.

Fucking bastard! Micah scrunched his eyes closed and coughed up a bitter sob as he hunched over and stamped the back of his hand against his forehead. Even now, as hurt as he was, he couldn't be angry with Jackson. Even though Jack had ripped his heart out, lied to him, and used him, it still felt like blasphemy to curse his name. Perhaps in time— not that he would live long enough—he would be able to hate Jackson, but not now. Not yet.

The freezing wind bit the tears that streamed down his cheeks. What had he done wrong? All he'd wanted was to love Jack and be loved by him in return. But Jackson had made it clear tonight that he had no love in his heart for anyone but himself.

"I never loved you, Micah," he had said.

Micah buried his face in his palms and sobbed as Jackson's declaration played on a repeating loop through his mind.

It didn't matter that Jackson had said the words almost from the beginning. "I love you," he'd said within days of the start of their relationship. Now the truth had come out. They had just been words to Jackson. Words without meaning. And Micah had never seen it coming. So thorough was Jackson's manipulation that even his thoughts had betrayed what Micah wanted to hear. And yet, all along, Jackson's words, as well as his thoughts—at least up until recently—had been lies. All of it. One big fucking lie!

Micah slammed his fist against the marble wall he sat slumped against.

"You want something from me I can't give," Jackson had said. "I never wanted this to be forever. I never wanted to be your mate." Then Jack had dropped the bomb Micah had seen rocketing his way for weeks. "I've met someone else."

Someone else. The human he had seen Jack with at Berlin. Who was probably fucking Jackson right now. Fucking him like some motherfucking interloper thieving away what belonged to Micah. That son of a bitch!

There was nothing Micah could do. Jackson had made his decision, as flimsy as that was. He had chosen, and his choice wasn't Micah. And Micah would honor that choice, even if it killed him. Already, he could feel the black hole opening in his soul, sucking away his sanity.

Pain. All Micah wanted was pain. Pain would take away his suffering. Pain would ease the ache in his heart and give the demon that came for him from the bowels of hell an offering to buy Micah more time. More time to…what? To what? There would be no getting Jackson back. So, what was it Micah needed time for? The answer remained hidden within the shadows of his mind, like some blurred memory he couldn't quite grasp. He just instinctively knew that he needed more time…for something. Something important.

He hung his head between his outstretched arms, which rested on his knees. Right now, all that was important was this. Nothingness. Emptiness. Tears that froze against his skin.

Jackson had left him. The unavoidable end had finally come. Micah's life was over.

CHAPTER 10

Tristan stepped out of the shower and wrapped a towel around his waist before heading back in to check on Josie. She had been fine at the king's holiday party on Christmas Eve, but yesterday, she'd gotten sick twice, and this evening she didn't look any better.

"Baby? You okay?"

She stirred from sleep and reached for the box of cookies beside the bed with a moan. Poor thing had lived off Nabisco Ginger Snaps and ginger tea for the last twenty-four hours in an effort to quell her nausea.

"I'm going to stay home with you today," he said, brushing her hair off her face.

"No," she said quietly. "You don't need to do that. I can—"

He shushed her, placing his fingers against her lips. "Yes, I do need to do that. Remember what I said last week? Besides, you need to rest."

She rolled her eyes and nibbled on the edge of a cookie. "I hate that you're seeing me like this."

"Baby, all I see is the most beautiful female in the world, and she's carrying my child. I think she's ravishing." He caressed her cheek.

She began to laugh, and then her eyes opened wide as she slapped her hand over her mouth, scuttled out of bed, and darted to the bathroom. The sound of her vomiting had Tristan shaking his head. Decision final. He was taking some time off.

After joining her in the bathroom and helping her get cleaned up, brush her teeth, and sip some water, he carried her back to bed. "I'll be right back." He secured the towel around his waist and went to the living room.

He was about to pick up the phone when it rang.

"Hello?"

"I need some time off." It was Micah.

"Yeah? What for?" Tristan drove his hand over his hair as he glanced back toward the bedroom. The last thing he needed was for Micah to take time off when he was leaving to tend to Josie.

"Jackson split."

Fuck. Tristan slammed his eyes shut. He'd been so concerned about Josie he'd forgotten all about Micah and his looming breakup. "Shit, man, you okay?"

"Fine."

Tristan didn't buy the nonchalance for a second, especially since this was Micah. "I'm sending someone to pick you up. You need to be in observation."

"No."

"Micah—"

"I said no. I'm fine."

Micah was clearly not fine. He sounded too calm for fine. But the last thing he needed to do was make things worse. If it was one thing he knew from spending a millennium with Micah, it was that once the guy made up his mind on something, no one would change it.

"You sure?" he said, afraid for Micah.

"Fuck off."

The line went dead, and Tristan held his phone away from his ear and scowled. He didn't care what Micah said, he would have Malek send someone over to check on him. He dialed in to administration and informed them he was taking a two-week leave, and then called Malek.

"Tristan, what's up?" Malek said.

"You're in charge," he said. "I'm taking some time off to be with Josie."

"Is she all right?"

He glanced over his shoulder as Josie groaned. "Morning sickness. It's bad. She's having a hard time keeping anything down."

"The doc'll have something to help with that," Malek said.

"Yeah, I know. I'm going to call him next."

"How long do you think you'll be out?"

Tristan shrugged. "I put in for two weeks, but we'll see how it goes. I'll play it by ear, but right now I just want to be here with her."

"I understand."

That was the good thing about Malek. He was straight and dependable. Maybe a little dry, and maybe even a bit too tame, but that was just how he handled his business after Carmen died.

"One more thing," Tristan said. "Send someone to check on Micah."

"Why?"

"Jackson left him."

"When?"

"He didn't say." Tristan didn't like Micah being out there alone right now. "Just make sure someone goes over and checks on him. The address of his private residence is in his file."

Malek didn't say anything.

"Malek?"

"Yeah. Got it."

"Okay. Thanks. I'll be in touch. Call me if anything comes up I need to know about."

"Will do."

He disconnected and returned to Josie. Her face was pale, and she looked miserable.

"What's wrong with Micah?" she said.

Josie had always held a soft spot for Micah. She was probably the only one who could get through to him on his worst days.

"Ssshh." Tristan stroked her cheek. "You don't need to worry about Micah right now, baby."

She arched one brow at him. Even as sick as she was, she

was still a demanding little fireball. "What's wrong with him?"

Tristan took a deep breath and bowed his head. "Jackson left him."

"Oh no." She placed her fingers over her lips. "Poor Micah."

"Poor Micah?" Tristan leaned down and kissed her forehead. "What about poor you?"

"I'll live." She patted his hand. "Micah might not."

"Malek is going to send someone over to check on him. If anything's wrong, he'll let me know. Now, I'm going to call the doctor about getting some anti-nausea medicine." He kissed her again, got up, and returned to the living room. He couldn't worry about Micah. Micah was Malek's responsibility now.

MALEK STARED AT THE PHONE. The time had come. He was about to lose his oldest and dearest friend, and as he'd promised, he would do whatever he could to protect Micah's final days so he could go out in solitude without dishonoring himself.

Being that his life had mirrored Micah's in almost every way since the day they'd met, Malek only hoped it meant his end was near, too. He was tired of holding up false pretenses and trudging through life as a wraith.

Please God, please. Let me be next.

But it wasn't to be tonight. Tonight he had a team meeting to run, and he had to announce that Tristan wouldn't be around for the next couple of weeks.

He grabbed his gear, locked up, climbed into his truck, and headed to AKM. Once there, he got situated at Tristan's desk and started reviewing the files.

"Where's Tris?" Ari said as he led Io in about thirty minutes later.

Malek looked up from his tablet. "Taking care of Josie."

The two nodded and sat down. "So, you're in charge now." Io sprawled in his chair, grinning. "How does it feel?"

"No different." To Malek, being in charge didn't feel much

different from being a regular enforcer. Not that it should. He wasn't going to be in his new role permanently, so he wouldn't get used to it, and he had no desire for promotion.

A strange male with long, blond hair entered the office, stopped, frowned, backed up to read the nameplate by the door, and took a step back in. "Isn't this Tristan's office?"

Malek eyed him. "Yes. Who are you?"

"That's Severin," Ari said, waving the new guy in. "Come on in. Grab a seat."

Malek remembered Tristan mentioning a new addition to the team and recalled the file he'd read on the guy a few days ago. "Welcome to the team, Severin. Tristan's taking a short leave. His mate's pregnant." He waved his hand as if his explanation was all Sev needed to understand the situation.

Severin nodded, glanced at Ari, and then took a seat on the couch against the wall.

"While we wait on the others, why don't you tell us about yourself, Severin," Ari said.

"Yeah," Io chimed in. "What brings you to Chicago?"

Severin cleared his throat and shifted awkwardly as he shrugged. "I just needed a change of pace. There's not really that much to tell, to be honest." He looked at his hands.

Malek got the impression that Sev wasn't comfortable talking about himself.

"You'll have to come with us to Four Alarm later," Io said. "It's where we all hang out. Lots of action, if you know what I mean." He waggled his eyebrows.

Ari shook his head at Io as Sev's cheeks turned pink. "God, Io. Let the guy get settled before you bombard him with the meat market." Ari turned to Sev. "You'll have to excuse Io. He's kind of got a one-track mind."

Sev shrugged and gave Ari a crooked grin. "No problem."

"But you should still come hang out with us. Just ignore this guy." Ari gave Io a shove. "He'll just get you into trouble, anyway. But you can hang with me while he's off with the females."

"As long as you're not with me." Io shoved Ari back. "Which you usually are, I might add."

Ari huffed out an awkward chuckle then frowned and looked away.

Trace chose that moment to saunter into the office, black skull cap pulled over his head and a matchstick hanging from his bottom lip. "Who are you?" He chucked his chin toward Sev.

"Name's Severin. But everyone calls me Sev." He held out his hand.

"Sev's joining our team," Malek added, noting the nickname.

Trace regarded Sev's outstretched hand, but instead of shaking it, he formed a fist and bumped the back of Sev's knuckles with it. "Hey. Welcome."

"Thanks." Sev glanced curiously at his hand.

Trace parked at his usual place against the wall and crossed his arms. "Where's Micah?"

As nonchalantly as possible, Malek shrugged. "You know Micah. Maybe he'll be here, maybe he won't." He met Trace's gaze for a split second, and Trace's eyes narrowed. "Let's get started."

SOMETHING WASN'T RIGHT.

Trace watched Malek closely, and it was clear he knew something was up with Micah, so why was he keeping it such a big secret?

Damn. This wasn't good. Trace needed to get out of there and go make sure Micah was okay.

Seconds ticked by at a snail's pace, and even though the meeting took all of five minutes, it felt like an hour. When Malek dismissed them, Trace beelined for an SUV then raced toward Micah's apartment. On the sidewalk across the street from The Sentinel, he gazed up to the eighteenth floor, where the blackness of pain and agony ripped the air like invisible lightning without the thunder.

It didn't take a physicist to realize Jackson had broken up with Micah. Motherfucker. That fucking little asswipe of a weasel. Trace had known this day was coming. He had bumped into Jackson at a bar a couple of months ago. He'd been bragging about his time with Micah and how he'd gotten Micah to flog him. "See, told you I could pull him out of retirement." The fucktard had no real feelings for Micah. He was just using him for bragging rights with his friends... as if Micah had been nothing but a bet. A goddamn bet!

Everyone knew the reputation Micah had as one of the most masterful Doms in the Chicago area. And not just a Master, but a Lord, no less. It was a title Micah had never entirely took ownership of, but one that, from what Trace had learned, fit Micah perfectly. Submissives still sought him, even though he'd been out of the leather scene for years. And even though Jackson wasn't a true submissive, he was what Trace called a leather whore. Someone who didn't live the life but enjoyed affiliating himself with those who did. The little bitch.

Trace snarled aloud before he could stop himself, and his right hand twitched. Shit, but he needed to get himself under control, and that male up there on the eighteenth floor was his ticket to making that happen. If Jackson had destroyed his only chance for peace of mind, Trace would hunt that little prick down and make him pay. Fucking hell, he would make that shit stain pay with his life, and he would take great pleasure in making Jackson suffer before squeezing the life from his heart.

MICAH PACED IN HIS APARTMENT, his heart aching. Jackson was gone. His life was over. He was a dead man walking.

As pain ripped through his soul, he slid the door open and stepped out onto the balcony. Cold wind whipped his hair over and away from his face, and snowflakes splattered his skin like tiny airborne missiles...stinging tears to match those that rolled down his cheeks.

The past few weeks had been building toward this moment, and he'd set everything into place. Malek would protect his privacy, and he had pushed everyone else away. No one would come to find him. No one would interfere with his demise. All he needed now was time, and then he would finally be at peace.

Peace. Something he hadn't felt in almost a thousand years. The new world had sprung up around him, technology had altered and reinvented life time after time, and the planet had become both a safer and a more dangerous place all at once. Land had eroded, rivers had dried into beds of dust, and the polar ice caps had shrunk. For all the metamorphosis the world had undergone, Micah had remained the same wounded soul he had been after Katarina's death. He seemed to be the one constant in a sea of change, but now was his time to erode. To wither into dust. To die.

Only a miracle would keep Micah alive, and Micah didn't believe in miracles.

It was time for him to say his final farewell. He was among the oldest vampires still alive, considered a young ancient. But as he stared over the lights of Chicago, closed his eyes, and listened to the city's heartbeat within the hum of traffic and rushed steps of pedestrians hurrying along the sidewalk, none of that mattered. He was lost. Utterly swept into darkness.

He had fallen into hell, and in hell he would remain until death stole him.

Soon, he would see his beloved Katarina again. To walk with her in the afterlife where their souls could spend the rest of eternity with one another. Would she be sad that he hadn't fulfilled his promise to survive, or would she be happy to see him again?

"I'll find out soon enough," he muttered into the night.

Yes, soon, for mighty Micah had finally fallen.

DID YOU ENJOY READING THIS BOOK?

If you did, please help others enjoy it, too:

Recommend it.

Review it at Amazon, iBooks, or Goodreads

If you leave a review, please send me an email at donya@donyalynne.com or message me on Facebook so that I can thank you with a personal e-mail.

ABOUT THE AUTHOR

DONYA LYNNE is the bestselling author of the award winning All the King's Men Series and a member of Romance Writers of America. Making her home in a wooded suburb north of Indianapolis with her husband, Donya has lived in Indiana most of her life and knew at a young age that she was destined to be a writer. She started writing poetry in grade school and won her first short story contest in fourth grade. In junior high, she began writing romantic stories for her friends, and by her sophomore year, she'd been dubbed *Most Likely to Become a Romance Novelist*. In 2012, she made that dream come true by publishing her first two novels and a novella. Her work has earned her two IPPYs (one gold, one silver) and two eLit Awards (one gold, one silver) as well as numerous accolades. When she's not writing, she can be found cheering on the Indianapolis Colts or doing her cats' bidding.

For more information on Donya's books or just to say hello, visit her on Facebook or swing by her website.

www.facebook.com/DonyaLynne

www.donyalynne.com

www.ingramcontent.com/pod-product-compliance
Lightning Source LLC
Chambersburg PA
CBHW020251150626
46552CB00020B/769